*postcard*
and other stories

# *postcard*

and other stories

*To John,
an ode to many solitudes!*

*Anik See*

Copyright © 2009 by Anik See

All rights reserved. No part of this publication may be reproduced, stored in a retrieval system, or transmitted in any form or by any means, graphic, electronic, or mechanical—including photocopying, recording, taping, or through the use of information storage and retrieval systems—without prior written permission of the publisher or, in the case of photocopying or other reprographic copying, a license from the Canadian Copyright Licensing Agency (Access Copyright), One Yonge Street, Suite 1900, Toronto, ON, Canada, M5E 1E5.

**Library and Archives Canada Cataloguing in Publication**
See, Anik
    Postcard : and other stories / Anik See.
ISBN 978-1-55111-925-0
    I. Title.
PS8587.E3466P673 2009        C813'.6        C2009-901435-1

**Freehand Books**
412 – 815 1st Street SW
Calgary, Alberta
Canada T2P 1N3
www.freehand-books.com

**Book orders**
Broadview Press Inc.
280 Perry Street, Unit 5
Peterborough, Ontario
Canada K9J 7H5
Phone: 705-743-8990
Fax: 705-743-8353
customerservice@broadviewpress.com
www.broadviewpress.com

Edited by Melanie Little.
Cover design and photograph by David Drummond.
Interior design by Anik See.
Digital preparation by Eileen Eckert.

Printed on 100% post-consumer recycled and FSC-certified paper and bound in Canada.

**Mixed Sources**
Product group from well-managed forests, controlled sources and recycled wood or fiber
www.fsc.org Cert no. SW-COC-000952
© 1996 Forest Stewardship Council

Freehand Books acknowledges the support of the Canada Council for the Arts for its publishing program.

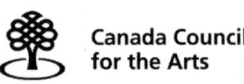

Canada Council   Conseil des Arts
for the Arts        du Canada

Freehand Books, an imprint of Broadview Press Inc., acknowledges the financial support for its publishing program provided by the Government of Canada through the Book Publishing Industry Development Program (BPIDP).

*for my father, for my mother, and for my sister*

binary  *11*

Ice Out  *29*

Etching  *57*

Kingwell  *81*

The Offing  *93*

postcard  *117*

binary

THE PLAN IS TO MEET at the boat at three to go sailing. I'm on my way. I'm on the streetcar and I'm on my way.

It's like this. I'm in the city visiting my brother. I live in a much smaller town, a little ways away. I teach high school there, in the very same high school where I won the Bob Tyrell Award three years in a row. Not that it matters, but just in case you're wondering who Bob Tyrell was, he was a mathematician. Not a great one, just some guy who decided to set up a scholarship at our school to encourage people like me.

He's fourteen years older than me, my brother, and he's a paramedic. Or was a paramedic, anyway. I'm not entirely sure what he does these days. Because of our age difference, we have a history of misunderstanding each other. Or rather, we let that fourteen years get in the way of understanding each other. Fourteen years is big. It's mid-generational. I'm too young to be his sister. He's not old enough to be anyone but someone between a brother and a father to me. We're more like second cousins once removed. Even now that we're adults, when you'd figure that an age difference wouldn't matter so much. That equation ($brother=sister+14$) is a funny thing. Two of the values are mutable, but the difference will always be fourteen. $Brother-sister=14$.

But I'm in town, and we're going sailing. I'm walking to the boat from the streetcar, walking towards the lake where the wind is blowing a breeze breezy enough that I wonder if we'll go out. I'm thinking of vectors, but more specifically I'm thinking of which vector will be the dominant one today — my brother's desire to sail or my brother's desire to drink — and in what direction the collision of the two will push us. My brother is a fair-weather sailor. Truth be told, he has the boat to sit on and drink. I'm not exactly sure what it is about sitting on a boat and drinking, but it sure feels good. Better than going to a place deliberately to drink. I mean if you go to a bar, you are going there to drink. If my brother is going to the boat, he can at least say out loud that he might go sailing. And then when he gets to the boat and the wind isn't absolutely perfect (or even if it is), he can say awwwww let's just have a drink instead. And sit on the boat, with it all tied up and the sails furled and the cobwebs shimmering between the sidestays.

 He goes out on the water about twice a year. But he said to me today "Meet me at the boat when you get into town and we'll go sailing, I promise."

 I'm at the boat now. It's three-thirty. He's not here. I'm looking out onto the lake again thinking there's no way we'll go out now. But still, I find a long-handled scrub brush in one of the lazarets and I'm standing at the middle of the boat on my tiptoes, reaching high up into the sidestays to swish away the cobwebs.

 I had a dream last night that Francis Ford Coppola came to the restaurant I go to, near my town. He ate and drank and then charged everything to me, which might have been all right if I'd been there. I wasn't there. The good news, the owner told me, was that it was only $272.93, which seemed quite reasonable for a man with such a consumptive reputation. On the other hand, to eat for almost three hundred dollars at that restaurant would be a lot of work. It's called a "bistro," but that's really just a fancy word for the best place to eat for miles around. Which isn't saying much, since it's also the only place for miles around. But in my dream the owner told me that there was more good news. He told me that John Cusack was in the restaurant at the same time (not with Coppola), so all was forgiven. And he paid for his own meal. When I'm mad at something, especially men, I think of John Cusack and I feel better. I know an astonishing number of women who do this. Once, I asked a male friend of mine who the guy's equivalent of John Cusack was. He looked up, hummed, hawed and stroked his new goatee. Then he said, "You know, I'm pretty sure it's John Cusack." I wonder if John Cusack knows he has that effect. I'm not thinking of John Cusack right now, but sometimes I wish my brother were him. That way I could never get mad at him. Somehow in the secularity of our never having been close there exists a hope that something will change, that how we are now and always have been is only a temporality.

*binary*

*distance = hope for temporality*

$$reality = \frac{permanent\ relationship}{distance}$$

$$therefore,\ reality = \frac{permanent\ relationship}{hope\ for\ temporality}$$

It's difficult to explain.
I walk up the dock to the clubhouse. There's a bar there. My brother's in it. He's been there the whole time, just didn't say anything, didn't try to get my attention when he saw me going down to the boat. I figured it was either that or he'd decided to stop somewhere on the way between his place and the boat. Which is only about half a mile, and which he drives. Gosh, a quarter of a mile seems a short way to drive for a drink, but he does it all the time. He's done it a bit too often, in fact. Paramedics are like pilots. They're not allowed to have a drink at least eight hours before their shift. But my brother's thirst is above regulation. His trajectory is always about the shortest distance between him and a drink. It's that old Hobbesian notion that all our emotions, actions and judgments are dictated by either appetite or aversion, i.e. increasing pleasure or avoiding pain. Or some combination of the two.

"Hey," he says, and waves.
"Hey." You want to go out?
He looks over his shoulder at the lake, crinkles his nose and shrugs. "Naw. Let's have a drink."
I pull up a chair beside him and order a beer. The last time I saw him was six months ago and I have no idea what to say now. I could ask him if he's found a job, if he's working, but every time I do so on the phone, he ignores my question. He doesn't change the subject, he's just quiet. Waits for me to ask him something else. So I do. Because, really, I care, but sometimes he makes it difficult. So it's just easier to let him win.
It's also like this: I'm an introvert but sometimes I get tired of my introvertedness and take drastic measures. I tell my brother that tonight I'm going to a club that happens to be playing a trance DJ that I like. It's the real reason I came to see my brother but I don't

tell him that. I'm not a trance scene freak. Someone just gave me this guy's CD and I like it. I tell my brother that the thing will probably go really late and that I'll just sleep on the boat instead of at his place, if that's all right with him. He never sleeps on the boat. No matter how much he's had to drink. So I know it'll be all right. Anyhow, when I tell him, he just looks at me silently, narrowing and widening his eyes. He orders another rum and coke. He looks away and doesn't ask me anything else. And I don't ask him anything either.

My brother's girlfriend and her daughter show up.

"Hey," he says.

"Hey," they say.

He picks up his drink and says to them "Let's go chase some geese." They walk away, down the dock. I hear him start up the engine on his dinghy. I finish my beer and walk back to the boat. They're speeding their way out into the bay. I sit on the boat listening to the distant engine whine back and forth on the water. I'm thinking about triangles — about trigonometry, specifically. You know, $a^2+b^2=c^2$. It's the study of the relations of the sides and angles of triangles and the deduction of certain components of those triangles. I'm thinking about him and her and me. I'm thinking about the functions of those angles, how they relate to each other. The engine is distant, sounds like a deerfly circling around my head. I can hear my brother and his girlfriend and her daughter yelping with something between fear and laughter.

They come back after about half an hour and the guy on the boat next to my brother's opens a bottle of warm champagne and passes it over the lifelines while it's still foaming out the neck. My brother puts his mouth over the top, catching most of it. He gulps a few times, laughing when the bubbles go up his nose. Then he holds the bottle out to me.

"No thanks."

"Aww, come on…"

"I'm fine with this," I say, holding up a glass of red wine he's just poured me. He starts to pour champagne into my glass anyway. I pull it away, put my hand over top.

"Just topping you up," he says.

He tops everyone else up, then keeps the bottle for himself, laughing as he drinks dramatically from it. Everyone else is laughing too. He does it again, and keeps doing it, even after we stop laughing. When the bottle's almost empty, he shoves it into his girlfriend's daughter's hands.

"Ewww... it's sticky."

"Try it," he says. "You'll get bubbles up your nose, like soda pop." She looks over at her mom, who says "Do it for uncle Don, honey." She tries to hoist it up, but it's too awkward for her. He places his index finger in the indent on the bottom of the bottle and helps her lift it to her mouth. She takes a bit and then tries to pull away, but my brother keeps pushing up on the bottle, until it's empty. She's got a mouthful now and it's pouring out of her mouth, getting all over her shorts and tank top. He's laughing. So's her mother.

"Gross," she says, when she's finally able to wipe her mouth dry. She looks down at her clothes and I get up from where I'm sitting at the back of the cockpit and go into the cabin to get her a towel. And a pop. My brother tells me to get him a beer. I tell him I'm not his maid. He tells me to get the fuck out of the cabin then, so he can go down and get one himself. I tell him he can ask nicely, pretending that the issue is about tone of voice.

We're having a conversation with the champagne guy, yelling between boats. We're nine people at this point. We sit around drinking for an hour or so, talking about nothing much. My brother graduates to straight rum and is trying to pour some into my glass of wine. It's still the same half-full glass that he tried to pour the champagne into. I let him pour it in, then put the glass down beside me and leave it there.

One of the women starts what I call the drunk-on-the-boat conversation.

"Harry," she says to the guy on the boat next to us, "did ya make it home OK last night?"

Harry thinks. "I woke up at home," he says. "Don't know how I got there though."

Everyone laughs.

"Attaboy." My brother.

"He," says my brother's girlfriend, jerking a thumb at him, "was so pissed last night he couldn't get it up."

"Ya, so what else is new?" says the other woman. "You're always complaining about that, and if it isn't that, it's about how smaaaaall he is." She and my brother's girlfriend shriek with laughter. Her daughter has her eye about an inch away from the hole in her pop can, inspecting the bottom with great interest like she usually does when her mother talks about my brother.

"Fucken stallion couldn't satisfy you," says my brother, grinning and taking a swig from the rum bottle, even though the glass he poured for himself is sitting right next to him.

"Honey, you ain't even close to a stallion," she says, holding two of her fingers up an inch apart, making sure everyone sees. And she and the other woman laugh again.

"Yah, well, you're no…" He stops. "It ain't the size of the pen, but the penmanship that counts," he says. He's not laughing now, and neither are Harry or any of the other guys.

"That?" she screeches, pointing to his groin. "If that thing were the size of a pen even, I'd be happy." She and the other woman are clutching their stomachs, shrieking again with that kind of laughter that feels really ugly. She is describing my brother's penis, and her nine-year-old daughter is sitting next to her. The men just sit silently, not looking at each other. I'm trying to shift in my seat, trying to pull my feet up from the floor of the cockpit, but it's sticky from the champagne that my brother poured all over his girlfriend's daughter's front and from all the drinks I kept putting my hand over. I've heard this conversation a hundred thousand times before and I'm doing everything I can to keep from holding my head in my hands. I mean I'm already doing it mentally, but I'm trying to stop myself from actually sitting there with my head in my hands.

I try to think of something else. But what pops into my head is one of my students the other day, asking me about a certain rate of conversion. When he asked, I stood there and stared at him for a little bit, then turned away and wrote the equation on the blackboard.

"Natural processes tend to go from an orderly state to a disorderly state," I told him. "It's called entropy. Crystalline solids are the most ordered of all states of matter, and therefore have the least entropy. Something in a gaseous state, something not quite black and white, say, something grey, or even varying shades of grey, exists almost totally in randomness and has the greatest entropy of all." Randomness is a hard concept for a lot of my students to grasp, because it seems immeasurable, unquantifiable. But it's funny how

*binary*

an equation can usually clear things up, even for something like disorder. So, I wrote it on the blackboard.

$$\Delta S_r^o = \Sigma \Delta S^o(\text{products}) - \Sigma \Delta S^o(\text{reactants}),$$

where $\Delta S_r^o$ is the entropy change in a reaction.

"Do you see what I'm trying to say?" I asked him. "I think so," he said, "but what does it mean practically?" "OK," I said. "Say you have three distinct layers of coloured marbles in a glass jar. If you shake the jar, all the marbles get mixed up, and the chances of shaking the marbles again and getting them back into those layered colours again is next to zero. That's entropy. It's basically another word for wasted energy, or a general decline into disorder."

He looked at the equation again. "That's a lot of variables," he said. He looked disappointed. I didn't know what else to say.

Nine p.m. My brother's swaying and slurring. Half an hour ago, he even drank the stuff in my glass, that mixture of red wine, champagne and rum. Didn't even flinch at the taste. Called it The Stallion and tried to mix another one, but spilled the last of the rum. So he put something else in. Called it something else.

When I get up and say I've got to head downtown, he kind of wobbles in his seat, looks at me, but doesn't say anything. Everyone else looks up, and just as I say goodbye, someone passes a bottle around and they're distracted. That holding the glass out and waving it about thing. The nine-year-old is inspecting the bottom of another can of pop. I tousle her hair and she looks up at me. "Bye," she says, and watches me when I get off the boat. I walk down the dock, sneakers squeaking, the soles resisting slightly each time I pull them away from the wood.

First I walk up to my brother's place to have a shower. I wash the wine off my hand. I call the club and find out that the DJ is on from 1:30 till 5:30 a.m. I flip through the channels on my brother's TV for a couple of hours until it's time to leave. Actually, I mostly just sit there, looking around his living room, which hasn't been dusted in months. Just as I'm getting ready, there's a loud crash at the door. An inordinate amount of key fumbling and lock fiddling. I open the door and my brother falls in. His girlfriend shortly after. Not fall-flat-on-your-face fall, but falling-down-drunk fall. My brother looks up at me from the carpet in his hallway and yells (not a mad yell, but a falling-down-drunk yell) I THOUGHT YOU WERE SLEEPING ON THE BOAT. I help them up and in. They're laughing. "I'm just on my way downtown," I explain, but they're already ignoring me. My brother is pushing his girlfriend past me. They're stumbling their way into the bedroom. Laughing. Groaning. The door to the bedroom slams shut. All of a sudden it's quiet.

I step outside and close the door. His car is parked on the lawn. Well, halfway. At an impossible angle, headlights on, blinding me. I walk over to it and shut the engine off. Pocket the keys. What strikes me most is that I've done this a hundred thousand times before. He gets very possessive of his car when he is drunk and it scares the crap out of me. It scares me because the probability that my brother will drive home drunk is always greater than his assumption that he'll be caught. That number, or the emotional value of that chance that he assumes, anyway, is very small, like $\frac{1}{\infty}$.

I'm mad. I'm mad. I'm mad at him. And I'm mad at me for not being able to say or do anything. But I'm pretty sure I'll have it all figured out by the time I get to Richmond Street. I'm on the streetcar. And my brother is either passed out or trying to have sex. The stallion.

It's 12:30 when I get to the club. Richmond Street is overflowing with beautiful people. I'm in jeans. A checked shirt. The beautiful people steer wide around me. Kind of feels like being on the boat. I came straight because I came alone. Or I came alone because I came straight. Whatever. Me and my beer and my half-glass of wine. And about three glasses of other stuff poured over my hand. That's clean now. There's a half-hour wait to get in. I wait half an hour and go in.

It's loud. I'm trying to think of the last time I was in a dance club and realize it's never. I mean, I've been to places where I danced, but they were extensions of bars, or small concert halls. Never a club specifically for dancing. There are a lot of people. The DJ who's spinning now feels OK. Not great, but OK. I know nothing about DJing. I'm just going on feel. The crowd seems to like him enough. He's not Max, the guy I came to see.

## binary

He spins for about an hour. I'm tired. Everyone around me seems to be having fun. No falling-down drunks. I'm standing off to the side, observing, thinking about my brother. Someone offers me a few puffs on a joint. I accept, holding the smoke until I feel it lift slowly through and beyond my eyes, into my head. Russell Banks says that with marijuana your inner life and outer life merge and comfort each other. He says that they merge with alcohol too, but they tend to beat up on you instead, and that people try to twist themselves into all kinds of weird shapes in order to deny what has happened. I try to put those two thoughts into equation form, but it's too hard here, without pen and paper. And really, it's all quite simple. I've lost my brother and I'm trying to find the shape that explains it. A figure eight, maybe, with me in one loop and him in the other. Joined only at a singular point.

We see things differently, I guess, my brother and I. Our father had a permanent seat in the local bar, the one in the town I now teach in, though no one holds that against me. And when we were young and my mother needed to speak to him, she'd send my brother there to get him. My brother was the star of the school wrestling team back then, and when he'd walk in there to try and collect him our father would look at him then shout that if my brother could pin down anyone in the bar, the manager would have to wipe my father's tab clean. It was an approval from my father that was conditional on my brother's winning; it was his only hope of getting our father out of there. My brother tells the story proudly, as if this was the very thing that inspired him to follow in his footsteps, or at least helped him choose to. To me, it's betrayal, using a child to get what you need done done. I go in that bar every once in a while, not to drink but just to see if I can imagine anything about our father, and mostly I come out of there sad that I have to go to a bar to try to piece him, of all people, together. Though I don't know that my being here tonight is all that different. Trying to piece together my brother. I still have Russell Banks on the brain, and while I'm looking around this place, I remember what he said about significant pain: that it isolates you, but sometimes, especially after a loss, it's all you've got — you have to use whatever's left, even if it isolates you from someone else.

The club is thump thumpy. The slide on the screen behind the DJ changes. Max. He starts spinning. The DJ before had a manufactured coolness — the kind of coolness that feels put on. Like a TV personality. Whereas Max feels just plain cool. All the time. He can't help it. He just is. The other DJ's music was tinny. Max's resonates with complexity. Depth. Whatever the sum of complexity and depth is. None of this has anything to do with the fact that Max is very cute. None of us is imagining this depth/complexity equation because we like to look at him. We love Max. He's a DJ's DJ. I think.

I'm slipping in and out of consciousness with the music. Whether it's exhaustion or trance, I don't know. It's my first time. There is a video of binary code and flickering alphabets, DNA sequences and fast, close-up skims along the surfaces of impossible buildings flaring on one entire wall of the club. I like the binary code. Streams of 1001000010010000011110100001010100101001010010000000011111 01010101010101001010101010101000000001010101011111101010001 0101000111010100100000110000000010101010010001010100101001 01110000010101011001101000101000000 flashing up vertically, 1s changing to 0s and 0s changing to 1s flash flash

The infinite possibilities of 0s and 1s spew out of the gunk-gunkgunkgunk of the music. I'm trying to figure out if what I'm witnessing on the dance floor is collective individualism or individual collectivism. Heads bob, each in its own beat. The occasional arm explodes above them, catching the split-second strobe of a light already twisting away towards another flash split-second point, like a washing-machine agitator on speed, broken from its foundation. At any given moment, there are a handful of people scattered through the crowd, each grinning their own grin, nodding violently when they grasp exactly how Max is mixing the music. A second later a different handful of people break into grins, grasping something different again, those things they like to hear, at what seems like a hundred thousand beats a second. Everyone's reaching into the music, which has already reached into us. We're reaching into ourselves, imploding, we think, and then BOOM there's an explosion, a new beat Max has brought up, and it brings us outside of ourselves, reaches away, unbounded, limitless, everything possible. There are twenty men for every woman. We are here. We are young. We are invincible. We sense some sort of power, a gestaltist power. A collective power greater than all of our own put together, because everyone who is here is thinking the same thing,

*binary*

as individuals, and there is no one else to say otherwise. At this moment. And the music is the embodiment of that collectivism, us circling around it, it circling around us, sort of like *enthalpy*, and we love it. A roomful of people feeling the same thing, every sensation made sharper by the music, and yet flowing into one seamless episode.

*binary combinations+music(implosion+explosion)=individuality$^n$*

*where n=the number of people in the room, and*
*the possibilities of binary combinations are infinite*
*and $i^n < p$*
*(where p=collective power of the individuals)*
*therefore, $i^n = \infty$*
*and $p = \infty$*

And somehow there's a randomness worked into it all too — in the music (why those pieces? what qualities do they have that make them weave together so well?), in the type of people here (why here? why tonight?), in their movements. I don't know how it all fits in. It just is. In this space, with this music, with this crowd. But we're only connecting in here. We wouldn't connect out on the street — probably wouldn't even recognize or acknowledge each other. Which is sort of the point. Because really, where's the truth in identity, beyond a truth that exists in a moment? Sharing something can eclipse it, in a good way.

The room is so smoky that when I close my eyes to listen to how the music is clicking in place, tears roll slowly down my cheeks. Someone wipes them away and asks if I'm OK. "Yeah, it's just the smoke," I say. Max looks up from his mixer. He looks at us looking at him, jumping and laughing, and he smiles. He drops his headphones around his neck and raises his long, beautiful arms. He grins and shrugs, as if to say, "I don't know what the hell it means, but it seems to be working." We roar. It's an instant where the possibility of possibility is overwhelming. It's tangible and undefinable at the same time. There is another explosion of beat and we're drawn outside ourselves again. There's a collision of sorts going on here, but I'm not sure of what. Something just slightly out of reach. It makes me light-headed. If I weren't so tired and leftover mad, this would be transcendent.

$$transcendence > \frac{music\,(implosion + explosion) + individuality^n}{anger + exhaustion}$$

Five-thirty a.m. Outside the club, everything a whisper. I walk along Queen for half an hour, until my bus comes and I step onto it, looking out the back window at the sky turning light pink in the east. I'm trying to remember the last time I deliberately stayed up all night. Five years ago, at least. The bus is stopped at a red light. The headline on *The Sun* is GENOA BURNS. A protestor was killed there yesterday. Up the street, there's a man in an abandoned parking lot, selling bonsai trees. At six in the morning. He looks very content, sitting on a wooden crate, just gazing at all the things around him. That's the thing with six a.m., that's the thing with the convergence of night and morning. You see and hear everything.

He sees me sitting on the bus, looking at him, and he looks back at me and smiles. In the thirty seconds that we stare quietly at each other, he suddenly seems to embody all that is concrete in impermanence. In that thirty seconds that pass between us, he makes graspable the impossibility that objects and ideas hold different meanings for every single person who looks at them or embraces them or explores them. An impossibility that's immeasurable, yet palpable in everything that surrounds him, and he, a man selling impossibly small trees from a concrete wedge in Toronto at dawn while Genoa burns, seems to be acknowledging that, letting go of his sense of self, letting the world work things in its own way and just absorbing it. The age-old intersection of possibility and actuality is what he is…

I doze here and there on the bus — a strobe doze. I get off at Park Lawn and walk through wet grass to the boat. It's bright now. A perfect wind is blowing. I think even my brother would go out sailing in this wind. I walk down the dock listening to robins chirping, and I climb down into the cabin, leave the companionway open and crawl fully clothed into a berth.

I sleep for about an hour and a half. And then I'm awake. Can't sleep anymore. Past the point of tired. I hear a noise in the front of

*binary*

the boat. It's my brother's girlfriend's daughter. She's rolling over in a sleeping bag.

"Hey," I say.

"Hey," she says.

"You OK?" I ask.

"Yeah."

"What happened?"

"I dunno. I guess everyone left."

Jesus.

"What time is it?" she asks.

"8:30."

"Oh."

My heart is pounding like mad and I'm trying to breathe, trying to sound normal. "Were you cold last night?"

"No," she says. "I found this sleeping bag."

"Did I scare you when I came down?"

"Nah," she says. And I smile at her.

"Good." I don't say anything for a while. Still trying to breathe normally. Then, "Come on. Let's get you some breakfast."

"OK," she says.

We walk over to my brother's. After about five minutes of us ringing the doorbell, he opens the door. He looks like crap. And probably so do I. I dig through my pockets and hand him his car keys. He looks at them, then at me. He leans forward to look out the door. When he sees the car half on the lawn, he says, "Is that a joke?" "I don't know, is it?" I ask. He throws the car keys on the table by the door and walks away.

I put my brother's girlfriend's daughter on the couch and go and get her a glass of juice, but by the time I come back with it, she's asleep again.

I'm shaking. My brother's in the kitchen, wearing only a pair of saggy, ripped briefs, having a glass of white wine while he cooks himself some eggs. I cross my arms in front of my chest, watching my brother shove the eggs around the pan with his spatula. He knows I'm looking at him, but he doesn't look over at me. He turns around and gets a plate from the cupboard. He pushes the eggs onto the plate and gets a fork from a drawer. He opens the fridge and pulls out a wine bottle. He fills his wineglass again and takes a big sip. He squeezes past me in the doorway with his plate and glass and goes and sits down at the table in the dining room.

"Daaaaaaarlin," his girlfriend moans from the bedroom. He looks up at me, takes a napkin and wipes his mouth, still looking at me, throws the napkin on the table, takes his wineglass, gets up and walks past me into the bedroom. He shuts the door.

I've had an hour and a half's sleep and I can feel tears running down my cheeks. No smoke this time.

This is crazy. It's reminding me of the time when I was eighteen and I tried to place conditions on my father seeing me, just after my mom left and I moved away from home. I said to him "I'll come and see you if you don't drink." His new girlfriend snorted at the suggestion. My father said he would see me and not drink. It was a long time ago. He saw me and drank. I thought that tension had gone away, but this morning I feel as though I've been slung back to it. I am thirty-two and feel like I'm eighteen again. It feels sudden, that resurfacing.

It's better when I don't say anything to my brother (like it was better when I didn't say anything to my father), and god you have no idea how much that bothers me. As unpredictable as his behaviour is, it's easier to keep the status quo when I'm doing nothing to provoke that behaviour. As unpleasant as that status quo is, I have a fear that anything I do to change it could make things even worse. Let me tell you why. Because suddenly I could be responsible for behaviour even more unpredictable on his part than I'm used to. And because he'd be provoked from the outside, he'd be in a situation in which he felt he had no control (and him not sailing, or having a girlfriend he doesn't love and who doesn't love him, or driving home drunk, those are all situations in which he feels he's in control), and all hell would break loose. It's not so much a judgment as it is a moral algorithm.

I should have just told that kid the other day that it's not all about science. That how much something hurts, say, like a cut, is one thing, but what it means in the end, how it affects us, what kind of scar it leaves, is an entirely different thing, and almost impossible to anticipate. That ultimately we're more defined by contrast than we are by a solid state of things. The thing I wanted to tell him most was that the hope things will change can be more destructive than the thing you want to change. *Quod erat demonstrandum.*

*binary*

The rest of the day is randomly surreal. I hear trance beats in the GO train zipping past me on the Gardiner. I have a few of these blackouts where I see flashing strobes of girls dancing instead of what I'm looking at. My brother's keeping his distance. I'm down on the boat again. I'm leaving early in the morning to go to my mom's. My brother and I are supposed to have dinner here together, in a little while, leftovers in the cockpit, probably shrouded in thick silence, but he's at the bar now, having just one more beer. In a while he'll come down to the boat, say that the people at the bar are going for Greek in a strip mall at the end of the road. He'll want to know if I want to come (*guilt* + *tension* = *obligation*). I'll say Another time, I'm not good company, because I know that someone will order a couple of bottles of ouzo and the drunk-on-the-boat conversation will become the drunk-in-the-restaurant conversation and when we leave I will have to go to the owner of the restaurant, or at least our waitress, who will have endured lascivious stares and pinches and lewd comments, and I will apologize. I will express embarrassment about my forty-six-year-old brother's behaviour. So I won't go to the restaurant. I've learned from experience. I'll say Another time. And he'll kiss me on the forehead and say Come up and see me before you go in the morning and Are you sure you don't mind if I go and I'll say Of course I don't mind and then he'll leave. And when he leaves, I'll sit out in the cockpit for a long time, wondering why it's so hard for us to be brother and sister, why I want to see a connection in him and why he won't see it, why it's so difficult for us to tell each other what we want.

Or for us to realize that really, we want the same thing.

My brother's name is Don. He is fourteen years older than me. I haven't got a clue who he is, because I don't share anything with him. Except blood. And time. And if fourteen were a prime number, that might explain why we don't get along. But it isn't. There are other factors involved.

It's raining now, the kind of rain with long, rolly thunder an hour before, then little drops that make you think Is that it? Then sheets of it, so much that it looks like wind on the water, all jaggedy lines, the drops dancing on the surface, violently. A single piece of hail falls into the cockpit.

I want to sit and watch the storm, but there's no good window on a boat for that, so I wedge myself into the companionway, rest my feet on the door jamb, watching, getting one side of me all wet, trying to figure this equation, doodling with numbers and fractals and the roots of things that seem simple. But there's nothing simple about it. There are no equal signs. It's all about inaccessibility, about a kind of refusal that is unquantifiable. Spinoza did it. He used geometry, or at least the deduction of it, to compose ethical guidelines. But I'm no Spinoza. I'm just someone sitting on a boat in the west end of Toronto. And Spinoza's guidelines, while pure genius, proved to be so inaccessible that they remain largely forgotten, and untaught.

The thunder isn't scary, not like the other night, when I dreamt of John Cusack and Francis Ford Coppola. It's close, but starts out small above me, quiet almost, then ripples down the bay against the rain, slowly getting louder, but past me already, swinging past all the other boats with people wedged in their companionways, watching.

The probability of being struck by lightning on dry land is about 1 in 1,000,000. On water, on a boat with a metal mast, that probability is reduced to 1 in 58,000.

It takes a long time for that piece of hail to melt.

I am tired. My whole body aches I am so tired. The rain has made a mess of my calculations; drops of it pull the ink from my fountain pen away from the page in strains, like the mare's tails in the sky now. I'll have to start over again in the morning, on the train to my mother's. I look up the dock at the bar. It's empty, closed, lights off. My brother did not come down to invite me out after all.

The rain is gone. The sky has cleared. The sun is setting, the moon looks pregnant. A beautiful evening breeze has picked up, and I don't know what to do.

## Ice Out

I LIVE IN A CABIN, near a lodge at one of the locks along the Rideau Canal, about halfway between Kingston and Ottawa. It's water-access only, and sits on a small island in the middle of Lake Opinicon, which is fine this time of year, which happens to be mid-December, because it means I can walk or snowshoe the half mile or so across the ice to the lodge where I can catch a ride into town to stock up on supplies. In the summer I take the canoe or the outboard, but there are a few tricky weeks in March, usually around the time when you set the clocks forward for Daylight Savings Time, and the end of November, when the ice is either forming or breaking up, and a boat won't get through but the ice isn't solid enough to hold 120 pounds of human, let alone a half-ton truck. A period of temporary immobility, strandedness. Around here, we call it ice out.

The lodge is open year-round but is busiest in summer, because the locks are closed from Thanksgiving till Victoria Day. In the winter, it's mostly snowmobilers and corporations who use the lodge, for retreats, or team building, old-timer reunions, slap-on-the-back get-togethers. The owners, the Morrises, have a few cabins scattered around that aren't associated with the lodge, and they rent them out to people like me, loners who need a cheap place to stay, and who don't bother anyone. Because the Morrises have lived here a long time, though, they know all about cabin fever, and so anyone who rents one of the cabins is encouraged to use the public areas in the lodge to meet other people and to stay sane while the snow is on the ground and the lakes on either side of the locks are frozen enough to drive across.

Unlike most people around here, I'm not from here. I'm from the city. Moved out here voluntarily. Now, you're probably thinking there are only three things that would make someone move from there to here willingly: 1. early retirement, which, in my case, would mean retirement before thirty; 2. involuntary assignment to a rural school board; or, 3. after years of trying to make it as an artist in the city, this was the only option of surviving — living simply, quietly, within one's means. Oh, and, 4. love. You might move here if you fell in love with someone who lived here. And with me, you'd be right on the third guess.

I'm a painter. And so far this place suits me. I picked it by pulling out a map, closing my eyes and sticking my finger on it. Imagine my delight when I lifted my finger and saw where it had landed. This is what city folk refer to as God's Country. Bucolic. Rolling green hills that give off the scent of fresh-cut hay. Ten thousand lakes and islands with plenty of places to catch rock bass, that special smell of the sun heating up fallen pine needles, loon calls at dawn. For months after I moved here, I wondered if my finger hadn't been subconsciously directed, like hands on a Ouija board, when you know what you want the answer to be, but you just need something seemingly random to tell you. To make it feel like fate, or destiny. Unlike most people around here who seem to have a genetic itch to get out but never seem to make it, I love this place, can't ever imagine leaving.

The cabin itself is perfect for a painter: old, lived-in and well-loved. It's got big, double-paned windows on three sides, a wood-burning stove, running water, electricity, a phone, all the amenities. The lodge is one of those places that was built in the '30s, and hasn't had a day's renovation since. It caters to a class of people somewhere between the old-moneyed and the nouveau-riche of Ontario and Quebec; the only people who use this place are a level-headed sort who've been coming for generations. It's too rustic to be called a resort. Not a golf club for at least a hundred miles in either direction, the heat in the rooms so random that it keeps the demanding people away, which is just how the owners like it. Occasionally, the Morrises will ask us to do a few days of work in exchange for cheap rent and a meal in the dining room.

I happen to be doing just that when I meet him. That's what this is all about. Picture me passing back and forth between the minus-thirty-degree weather outside and the fireplace inside, filling the woodbox, while a group of men about ten, fifteen years older than me sit talking. The first time I pass him, he looks up and I feel his eyes following me. I dump the wood into the box, turn around and walk back outside. Fill my arms with wood again. I pass him, he stands up, mid-sentence, asks me if I need help. His eyes are henna green, and they lock in. I feel my lips moving, acutely aware that there are some things you just can't fight. Say No thanks. He smiles, says OK. Sits back down. I go outside, stack more wood in my arms, the cold sticking to me like honey, slowly softening when I go back inside, fill the box one more time. Tall, dark and handsome. Six-foot-four, black curly hair and sallow skin. Like Vince Vaughn, only cuter, even. Kinda goofy. But thinks he isn't.

At dinner, he sits at the table directly behind me. I'm at the staff table, even though I'm not really staff. He's having a conversation with someone else at his table and I'm close enough to listen, but I don't do that. I'm looking outside, staring at a skimpy snow that's started to fall, asking Mrs. Morris how that can be possible in such cold. She starts to answer, in her typical Mrs. Morris way, which is to shake her head ambiguously, wonderingly, before releasing a slow-worded response. Halfway through it, there's a clattering of cutlery beside me. He's brought his plate over, sits down, says to me, And what are you doing up here? I look at him. Self-imposed exile, I say. Mrs. Morris laughs, pats me on the shoulder with her old, wrinkled hand as she gets up and leaves. I put a small piece of bread in my mouth. Chew it while I watch his face. He turns to the window and looks out at the snow for a moment. And laughs.

He's here for a corporate leadership retreat — that's all he says about that — divorced, three kids, the oldest of which (twelve) is here with him, he says, though I never meet him. Four days of looking at recommendations made in point form on an overhead projector while the cold snap outside refuses to correct itself. Three nights.

So at dinner each of these nights, he ignores his colleagues, joins me at my table and summarizes those points (*prioritize, delegate, communicate, revisit*), while I summarize the sky in weather like this (*three-dimensional blue, quiet and crystalline, like you can reach up and grab something infinite*), because he hasn't seen it all day, and by the time dinner rolls around, it's been dark for a couple of hours already.

We also talk briefly, shallowly, about things we know, leapfrogging onto lily pads of topics you need to talk about before you feel like you have a sense of someone, but which, in fact, don't really tell you anything about him. He tells me that he was at a dance club in Ottawa the other night, and wonders aloud about Chicago House, and I tell him that it started because of an inadvertent multicultural after-hours scene. Different "gangs" wanting to party and winding up mixing together, fusing their music in the process. He seems impressed but doesn't ask me how I know. I tell him anyway, that I grew up in Toronto, lived there till a couple of years ago, that as an artist you tend to get drawn into those scenes more intensely than most people. He looks away, then changes the subject to being an altar boy in a small town in Quebec in a Catholic church, when the United church across the street seemed to have things figured out in a much saner manner. Like what, I ask. Like marriage, or family, he says. But, he says, I was eleven, I couldn't switch. And then he starts telling me how he took his son to Morocco last summer to plant the travelling seed in him and asks do I think it's as impossible as he does to spend the rest of your life with one single person.

I tell him that I'm spending the winter up here painting. He looks off at something when I say this, and I picture him envisioning me working at the kind of sloppily detailed landscapes you see at garage sales, or in basements. But I don't say anything. He interrupts to tell me about the only car he has, a rare, right-hand-drive Aston-Martin. It's blue. He doesn't say what kind of blue — light, dark, aquamarine.

I don't want to give you the wrong impression. We're not as interested in each other as we appear; we're both more concerned with trying to place opinion, with presenting ourselves in a context that might be attractive to the other person. That much is apparent right off the bat.

On his last night, we're out for a walk on the lake, and even though there's a full moon it's a little too dark to see the blackness of the water under the ice. It's just about turned opaque now anyway, the ice, which makes me trust it more than the first few weeks after it freezes, when you can still see through it and you realize that really, you're standing on water.

I invite him back to my cabin to warm up. We walk in, and I go over to the stove and light it. It's not too cold inside; it's still warm from the fire I had going this afternoon, but I put another couple of logs on anyway, and boil some water for tea.

He looks around, sees the paints, seems a little surprised, says Show me something. I have paints all over my cabin, but when I'm not actually painting, I tend to turn the piece I'm working on towards the wall. I don't like looking at them when I'm not thinking about them. It's a one-room cabin. It's disruptive. So I go around the room, picking up my brushes. I gather them in a bunch, their big wide bristles pointing up, splayed like peacocks' tails, and I put them in his hand. He looks at them for a moment and seems confused. He runs the palm of his hand over their tops and they fling back into shape. He smiles, like he gets what I'm trying to tell him. Abstract? he asks. Then he picks one of the brushes and pulls it out. He holds it and brushes my cheek with it, lightly.

Where's your son? I ask.

Not here, he says. I raise my eyebrows, a little shocked at the enthusiasm in his tone. I don't know, he says, sleeping, I guess.

So I go over to the sink and look under it for an old coffee tin. I fill it with water and dig through my paintcase for an old, cracked set of watercolours. He stands behind me, watching, the bouquet of paintbrushes still in his hand. I pick three different sizes of them, and when I take the rest of them from him to put them away, his hand follows, as if he doesn't want to let go. I look around the room, look up at the light. I pull him over a few steps, stand back, look at him. I smile. He tilts his head, narrowing his eyes a bit, and tries to smile back.

I go over to him, place my hands on his chest. I undo the buttons on his shirt quickly, run my hand over his chest up to his shoulders, push the shirt off them and down his arms. He shakes his wrists and it accordions around his feet. I kick it away. I put a finger near his belly button, walk around him, looking at his skin and trailing my finger on it, looping around him as though tracing a line where I want to make an incision. I often do that when I'm studying something I'm going to paint. It helps me focus.

I stand in front of him again, my arms crossed over my chest, staring at his. Perfect. Creamy white. Small pores. Flat nipples like tiny sand dollars. I reach out to touch one, run my finger over it. He draws in his breath and I look at his arms. Goosebumps. I walk around him again, notice his nipples raised now.

I sit on a table across from him, just out of reach. I ask him to take his pants off. I look at his face when I do, see his eyes get a bit bigger in a way that says he doesn't want me to see his eyes getting bigger.

I'm not wearing any underwear, he says.

I'm still looking him in the eye — henna green. I shrug. I get off the table, walk around three walls of the cabin, turning down the blinds. Not that there's anyone to see anything. Better? I ask, and turn back to him. His pants are off. And he's just kicking his socks away. I guess so.

He has thick thighs, with dark hair that swirls in circles along his quadriceps. Penis stiffening and wavering slightly. He plants his feet a little farther apart, crosses his arms across his chest, looks me straight in the eye, following me as I move towards him. I take the arm that's on top, pull it from between his other elbow and stomach, place it by his side. He lets the other arm fall away. Stops looking at me. Penis flaccid.

I go over to my bed, turn my back to him, unbutton my jeans, slide them off. I dig around in my laundry pile for a pair of olive-green parachute pants. They're my painting pants. Why don't you just leave tho... he says, but I turn around and look at him and he shuts up. I put the pants on. I go back over to him.

He's quiet. I pull myself up onto the table, sit facing him, legs apart like his, and mix some paint. Sort of a sienna brown. I glance up at him and then look back down at the paint. Glance up at him again.

I dab in a bit of black, look up at the light, nod to myself. Do I have to be still? he asks. No, I say. Not at all. He doesn't move. I smile, almost start to laugh. Just relax, I say. I'm not going to hurt you. And then I go over to him with my brush by my side and I put my thumb on his cheek and I kiss him. I keep my lips still on his for a while, feeling the thickness of his lower one, the faint pulse that beats through it.

He brings his hands up, like he's going to run them through my hair, but I put my hands on his wrists before he does, slip out from under them. I go over to the table and pick up the palette. I dip the brush into the colour I mixed. I turn around, lean forward a bit and run the brush along the top of his first rib. He starts.

I flick my eyes up at him. Don't worry, I say. It's only watercolour. Oh, he says. I look back down at his stomach, paint a thin line just under his pelvic bone, then take my finger and smudge it a bit, so it blends in with his white skin.

Sort of like war paint, he says. No, I say. Yeah, I guess you wouldn't use brown for war paint, would you? he asks. I don't know, I say. I lean forward and paint his nipples browner, fill in his collarbone. Why brown, then? he asks. I had a lover in India a while ago, I say, and ever since then I can't get the shading of his skin out of my mind. I go back over to the table to mix some more paint. The colour of his skin? he asks. No, I say, the shading. The different layers of darkness and lightness. How they'd change when the light came from a different angle. Have you ever walked around a Persian carpet? I ask him, dipping my brush in the water. Yes, he says. And did you notice how the whole pattern changes when you do? Yes, he says, as a matter of fact, I did. Like that, I say. Just like that. But with skin. With a real live person. Hmmm, he says, and doesn't speak anymore for the rest of the night.

★

Three weeks later he calls to say he left his copy of *Gravity's Rainbow* at the lodge. I say I know, that I have it and that I read it in the meantime and that Pynchon always confuses me. He's quiet for a moment, then asks where I am. My cabin, I say. And then he apologizes for not calling sooner. I assumed the number you gave me was the lodge's main number, he says, and every time I thought about calling you it was after office hours. That's OK, I say. So about the book, he says. Come on out, I say.

A few nights later, the night after he says he'll be here, I look out my window and see a pair of headlights creeping across the ice towards the island, following the Morrises' tracks from when they were out here a few days ago, just checking up on things, making sure I had what I needed and that I hadn't started talking to the walls or skinning small animals. It's been cold for the past couple of weeks. A lot more snow has fallen. Enough that cabin fever has set in with the locals a month earlier than it usually does. Mr. Morris calls it hyper-isolation. Where you feel so housebound you want to tear a wall down, even though it's minus twenty-five out. Remember Peter Harris? he said, looking at his wife. She nodded, looked at me and said It's true, and thank god his kids were with their mother that weekend. The Morrises found him naked, frozen to the shore in front of his house. He had an axe in his hand and they figured he was trying to chop a hole in the ice so he could go swimming. He lived on an island too. Which is why the Morrises make a point of checking up on us cabin renters every now and then, in person.

In any case, it's still cold the night I see the headlights. Been dark for hours. It's him, a two-hour drive from where he told me he lives. I imagine it's somewhere around nine o'clock. He has two bottles of red wine and a six-pack of beer. You've got big plans, I say, what if I'd been working? Weren't you working the last time I was in here? he asks. I smile and let him in.

I open one of the bottles of wine while he takes his jacket off, sits down, looks around the cabin. It's quiet out here, he says, you can't even hear the water. It's frozen, I say. You just drove over it.

I give him his glass of wine. Neither of us says anything for a while. We sit and sip. So how come you know so much about house music? he asks. I paint to it, I say. It helps me focus. Good beat, no lyrics. It kind of pulls me along. He nods. Yeah, not too many people know the history of it, he says. That's why I asked. I go to clubs every once in a while, once a month, I guess, sometimes once a week, depends on what's going on. You know. Yeah. Ecstasy. It's a pretty neat thing. Well, except for the depression afterwards. That kind of sucks. But the beats — oh man. And sex. Sex on ecstasy is unbelievable. He looks at me.

I tilt my head. I thought sex on ecstasy is almost impossible, I say. I was under the impression that it's pretty tough to get an erection while you're on it, I say. His eyes widen and he shakes his head. Nuh-uh, he says. Not this soldier.

He takes a sip of wine. Do you want to do some? he asks, reaching for his pocket. Not now, I say. He nods his head, looks around the room.

Do you? I ask him. He shakes his head slowly, while still looking around the room, as if he's considering something else. OK then, I say. I think of his son — the twelve-year-old who was up here. The word "incongruous" comes to mind.

Are you on something right now? I ask. He looks over at me and laughs. No, why?

Just nervous then? I ask. He keeps looking at me. Look, you don't have to stay if you don't want to, I say. I won't be offended if you just want to pick up your book and go.

No, he says. That's not why I came out.

I'm just saying that if you change your mind, I won't be offended.

He nods slowly to himself. He looks over at me, runs his hand through his hair. So, he says. Can I paint you?

Paint paint, you mean?

No, he says. Like you painted me.

I smile and shake my head.

Why not? he asks.

I don't know. Be original. Ask me something about something instead. Start a conversation, I say.

Why? he says.

And he's right. We threw protocol out the window the instant we met.

Humour me, I say, just for the hell of it.

OK, he says. He gets up, comes over to me, takes the glass of wine from my hand. Can I stay over?

Sure, I say, shrugging. I pick up a brush and a couple of tubes of oils. He grabs my hand. The wine in the glass in his other hand sloshes, some of it hitting the floor. Slap. No, he says. No paint this time. I'm looking up at him, our faces are an inch apart, and I whisper, hard, *I was just putting them away. So they don't dry out.* And his face softens and I pull my hand away from his and he lets go at the same time.

So tell me something, I say. I put the oils away, turn the canvas I was working on towards the wall.

What do you want to know? he asks.

What was the best thing about your divorce?

The freedom.

And the worst?

Um... desperation... random desolation, I guess.

Well. Those are pretty quick answers.

They tend to be the things you think a lot about when you get a divorce.

So why'd you marry her?

I don't know, he says. She was cool. Now she's not so cool.

Come on. It's not that simple, I say.

He looks over at me. Starts unbuttoning his shirt. Maybe I just want it to be, he says. Anything wrong with that?

You mean you want it to be that simple whenever you think about it, or you want it to be that simple here, right now? I ask.

What difference does it make, for you? he asks. Why worry about it? It's my deal, not yours. He lies down on the bed.

I lie down beside him. We're on our sides, facing each other. I start mentally tracing the places on him that I painted before. My eyes skim over his shoulder, where the light behind him is kind of haloing it. The edge of his skin is blurry with brightness. He puts his hand in my waist, moves it to my belly button, starts to undo the buttons on my jeans. Do you mind if we do this? he asks. I shake my head.

OK, he says. But don't say anything. Just… No more questions, all right? And then he leans in and kisses me for the first time. Feels nice. Not sparky, or electric, but nice. Warm.

★

I wake up. Squint my eyes into a beam of sunlight that's shining on the bed, feel him beside me, hear him snoring lightly. I reach blindly beside the bed for the glass of water I usually keep there, but knock over a wine glass. Shit, I whisper, and try to grab it, but it clatters hollowly, musically, and does not break. He doesn't move. The wine glass is empty. We finished the bottle, but I'm still mostly dressed, and so is he.

I swing my legs off the bed, plant my feet on the cold wooden floor, hold my head in my hands for a split second and then get up. I walk around the cabin a couple of times. I fill the coffee grinder with some beans. I sit in my armchair and let my arm make a subconscious, circular motion. Get lost in thought, like I usually do before coffee, thinking about how diffused our purpose became, and how it softened the later it got. I gave him what I wanted, and I think he did the same. And they happened to be the same thing. Which was what, exactly?

The coffee grinder gives and the handle spins away from my hand. It's done. The coffee is ground. I put the coffee grinder on the table.

## Ice Out

Crawl back into bed, wanting to sleep some more. He's on his side, back to me, still snoring. He feels me beside him again, reaches back and strokes my thigh. Finds my arm and wraps it around him.

I run my fingers over his nipples. He reaches for my thigh, pulls it over his, then brings his hand up to the waist of my jeans, slips it between them and my skin. His fingers drift over my buttocks, linger between the small of my back and the dimple just above the crack. He rolls over, sleepily, faces me, opens his eyes, pushes me onto my back. Kisses me, pushes slowly, rhythmically against me, even though we both still have our pants on. He stops. Lifts my shirt and presses his bare chest against mine, as if desperate only for warmth, or for some sort of contact.

We sit up. I try to undress him, but he won't let me, pushes my hands away, and so we undress ourselves, then fall back into position. He's thick, uncircumcised, moving against me. There's no seduction. He doesn't stroke my body like you'd expect someone to when they marvel at nakedness as a new-found extension of someone they've only known clothed. But he makes sure that I come before he lets me do anything to him. Even then, I feel like I'm on the sidelines, watching, despite the fact that I'm directly involved.

I smile at him. His face is serious, but his eyes are vacant, not noticing the expression on my face. I want it to feel more satisfying than it does, keep trying new things, wondering if it's just me feeling this. Finally I quit trying, let him take over.

He immediately pushes me onto my back and the distance dissipates. Suddenly he's extraordinarily *present*. His desire tangible. I'm arched, halfway off the bed, and he's directly over me, pressed up against me, an inch from my face, looking right at me. I smile again. He smiles back this time, pushing fully into me.

We both shout when we come, and he collapses all of his weight onto me so that we fall off the bed. We lie laughing for a while, until he starts to shiver, and I reach up and pull the covers from the bed over us. I run the tips of my fingers up and down the valley of his spine, but he doesn't do anything back, falls asleep again on top of me. I slide out from under him without waking him. Then I fall asleep again too.

A couple of hours later I'm up, experimenting with some egg tempera. He wakes up. Hey, he says, looking out the window. I have my back to him, wave my brush at him. There's coffee on the stove, I say. Perfect, he says. But it's really strong, I say. If you want it weaker, just boil some water.

He gets up, puts his jeans on, pours himself a cup. Starts walking back to the bed. Is there any left? I ask. Yep, he says, think so. He sits on the bed, props some pillows up against the wall, leans back, pulls the covers over his knees. Looks out the window and takes a big sip. I get up from my painting, go over to the stove and pour what's left into my cup. It's quiet, inside and out.

Just thinking about last night, he says. His voice crisp, clean, straight through the cabin to me. Yeah? I ask, mine diffused, directionless, everywhere. Yeah, he says. It was nice.

Yeah, it was nice, I say.

And then he stands up, puts his shirt on, takes his book and leaves. He gives me a hug at the door. Doesn't say anything. Neither do I. He drives away in a Buick with Saskatchewan plates. Back across the ice, in daylight now. No questions.

★

He gave me his cell number, and I try calling it a few times, but I get a recording that he's unavailable. At the lodge, I look in the Ottawa white pages. He's there all right. Esterhazy, Nathaniel ("...and don't ever call me Nate," he said when he told me his name. "I hate that."). No address. A phone number different from the one he gave me. I write it down and wait till I'm back at the cabin to call it. A Bell operator recording tells me his number has been changed to the cell number he gave me.

I don't know why I'm calling, or what I want to say to him. Just have a conversation. I feel like I need to give him something about me that he could care about, that would solidify his idea (or mine) of my character, maybe.

I've thought about what my answer would be if he asked me about my relationship with my dad, or if I think artists should suffer for their art. Or if I'd go back to school. I'd tell him yes, I would. I'd like to do a master's in psychology. And I picture him asking psychiatry or psychology? and I'd answer psychology. He'd ask me why and I'd say because I'm not so much interested

# Ice Out

in prescribing drugs to fix a problem as I am interested in the dysfunctional behaviour itself. Typical artist. But, of course, that question would succeed him asking me where I went to school in the first place, and he hasn't asked me that yet. Nor have I asked him. I haven't asked him who he works for now, and he, aside from the first evening, hasn't asked to see any of my paintings. The only solid thing I know about him is that when he was in his early twenties, he was a brakeman on the railway that ran through Medicine Hat. And that he saw three co-workers cut in half, on three separate occasions, when they got caught between shunting railcars. That he had to go and pick up pieces of them. That he liked his job on the railway, but that his wife made him quit when she got pregnant because she wanted him to be responsible. That he is divorced and has three children, one of whom is a twelve-year-old boy. And that he hates what he does now (whatever that is). Everything else I know is opinion, mutable. Capricious, even. Controlled by him in what he tells me, uncontrolled in what I imagine about him.

He never talks about his kids. I don't even know their names. The last time he was here, he told me that he had a vasectomy nine years ago and then asked if I wanted to have kids. I told him that I waffle on the subject, and that makes me think I shouldn't have any. He said that sounded like good logic to him. I've decided that I'm just not going to get involved with anyone where it doesn't feel right, he said to me then, there's just no point. And I wondered if he was saying that to help me realize something he couldn't say more bluntly, or if he was just talking to himself; wondered what side of the equation I fell on, even though I knew.

He eventually calls, a few days after I look up his number at the lodge. He's on a land line, loudly sipping something with ice cubes in someone's house, maybe even his own, listening to the CBC in the background. When I tell him that the Morrises have just pulled up and I need to talk to them because the chainsaw is being temperamental again, he doesn't offer me the number. He says How long do you need? and that he'll call me back. And he does call back after the Morrises are gone, but just to say that he'll call me later in the week, that he's sorry, but his cellphone is broken. The ice cubes rattle in his glass just before he hangs up.

★

Occasionally, when I go over to the lodge, they'll have a stack of magazines and newspapers for me that the guests have left behind. They collect them when they're cleaning the rooms, and then they sift through the stacks, divvying them up among us residents. The guy in the cabin closest to me (he's on the mainland), a phys. ed. teacher at the high school in the next town over, gets all the *Sports Illustrated*s, and the young, pregnant girl who works in housekeeping gets all the fashion and wedding ones, though there aren't too many of those left behind in winter. What with snowmobilers and all. I get stuff like *The Atlantic Monthly, Harper's*.

I'm flipping through a three-month-old *New York Times Magazine* when the phone rings. It's him. About two weeks since that last time he was here. He says he's on the highway, heading south and west towards me. Asks me if I still have that other bottle of red wine. Yes, I say. Why, would you like some of it?

While I wait for him, I read an article about love of varying kinds: fifty-plus years of marriage, affairs, a same-sex marriage where one of the spouses decided to have a sex change afterwards: one day they were a lesbian married couple, six months later they were not. The article is prefaced by a page of six randomly taken photos, each of an allegedly married couple sitting across from each other in a dingy restaurant. They're all ignoring each other. The article says something about desire being contained in fulfillment, how there's no such thing as having desire without wanting fulfillment, or wanting fulfillment without having desire.

I think about all that distance between people, how it starts out as presence and slowly changes into its opposite, how we notice it happening and don't do anything about it for fear of changing the status quo (even though the status quo is changing), and how we convince ourselves it's not, even when we know it is. How he seems to have the ability to be both present and distant at once with me, sexually and otherwise. Present when talking about himself non-abstractly, on topics he brings up, and distant when answering questions that I ask him, never saying anything, not even my name, during sex or foreplay or after.

He comes in, doesn't say a word, pulls the magazine from my hands, throws it behind him. Grabs me and pushes me against the wall. Holds my hands in his and splays my arms across the wall. Kisses me hard. Unzips his pants. Rips open the button fly on my jeans. We fuck.

But I don't stop him when it doesn't feel like anything at all. I'm not sure why. It's unsettling. Again I want it to feel more satisfying than it does. It's almost as though he suspects his intention is transparent, so why bother with facade? The grace of illusion is relinquished, and the lack of meaning behind it starts to shine. There's no regret, or resentment, that there's nothing more. There's just no *knowledge* about the other person. It's curious. Odd, I mean. Bare.

But, I remind myself, a lie, if found in a genuine action, can be as truthful, revealing, as the truth. And can become truth, or at least glance off it, in its authenticity.

Did your wife remarry? I ask him later. We're in bed, naked, tired. I'm running my finger up and down the inside of his forearm. He's told me before that it tickles, but lets me do it anyway.

Mmmmmmm...

How does that make you feel?

I don't know. OK.

Has she been with him since she left you?

Mmmmmmm...

What's he like? What's his name?

I don't really know. He looks at me. Doesn't really matter, does it?

There's a *kwukkwukkwuk*, outside, low like a grouse, but sharper.

What's that? he asks.

It's a loon.

It is not.

Yes, it is. I guess they're on their way back. When they fly, they have a call that's different. In the winter, it's the only sound they make.

Get out.

I'm serious. It's a loon.

Huh.

★

If you fall through ice and get swept past the hole you fall through, you should try to flip yourself on your back and bring your face up to touch the ice, because there's a small air pocket between the ice and the water that's not frozen yet.

I heard that from a guy who used to hunt harp seals in Newfoundland, before it started to fuck him up. He said the worst part about it, about falling through ice, he meant, was the salt. The salt was more concentrated in water that was close to freezing, and so keeping your eyes open while you tried to find the air pocket, while you tried to inch your way back along the undersurface of the ice to the hole you came through, was almost impossible. But, he said, it kept you from thinking about the layer, almost see-through, that was holding you under.

At least here we don't have the salt to worry about.

★

How's the weather there, he asks. It's fine, I say. And it is. The ice is finally starting to break up. But not like on the rivers I'm used to. There's no pile-up. The lake rises and the ice just sinks under it a bit. Gets all slushy and suspends itself.

It doesn't make any noise, I say. The only noise I hear these days is the ice on the roof cracking. Icicles falling off.

He's on his cell. I can hear him breaking up. I ask him if he's on his way here. He says yes, he just drove through Merrickville and he's about forty-five minutes away now. I tell him to park at the lodge and walk over. The ice isn't strong enough to hold a car anymore. He's quiet then, like he never thought of that. If you come over, I say, you have to be prepared to be stuck for a couple of days. You realize that, don't you? It's ice out. And then his phone cuts out.

He comes in, we engage in some rigmarole: kiss a lot first, start to take each other's clothes off — he takes off my bra, and *then* my shirt — but then he stops. And I let him. We have a glass of wine, eat something. Lie on the bed beside each other after.

He asks me about my father. He was an alcoholic, I say. Did I already tell you that?

No... what was he again? A ski jumper?

Track athlete.

Right. Shot put.

High jump.

Right. (He thinks for a bit.) But... he's not a high jumper anymore.

I laugh. No. He's almost sixty.

## Ice Out

He shifts, says something about how I must have got my father's body. Because it's androgynous.

Most people just say it's thin, or muscular, I say.

I don't mean it as an insult, he says, or to say that it's not sexual. But he doesn't say that it is.

He asks to see my hands, says he has a theory that seems to get stronger with every person he tests it on. He says his theory is that moons in the fingernails mean androgyny in women, and maleness in men. He tells me that my moons are even more prominent than he assumed they would be. He says that they're a sign of testosterone and I'm a little taken aback, wonder if I should shatter his theory by acting more feminine. When I take his hands and look at his thumbs, he tells me that thumbs don't count.

Are you obsessed with androgyny? I ask.

He laughs, says, I guess so.

I want to know why.

Oh, I don't know, he says. Because that's the way I am, he says.

Obsessed? I ask.

Androgynous, he says.

In the morning, as I'm grinding coffee in my armchair and he's lying on his back, eyes open, shifting his body to follow the beam of sun over the bed, I ask him about his mother.

Oh, she died ten, twelve years ago, he says.

I laugh. Which was it? Ten or twelve?

I don't know. '88?

So, thirteen.

Sure.

How old was she?

I don't know, fifty-eight?

It always amazes me when people don't know their parents' ages.

Does it matter? It's just a number.

I guess birthdays were always a big deal in our house.

Oh.

Another reason to celebrate.

Oh yeah, he says, I know those nights. Those, and New Year's. He shudders. My mother lost her licence because she was driving drunk, he says, and the day she got it back, she wanted to go out and celebrate that she got it back.

Did she?

Uh huh. She wanted my dad to drive her, but he wouldn't. So she did. Drove to a bar thirty miles away. Celebrated. Drove back.

We both look out windows. No noise inside the cabin. Just the ice on the roof shifting and melting onto soggy ground. Splat, splat, splat. The sound of the sun heating things up. The sound of spring approaching, like a front, in a big, long line.

Is that coffee ready yet? he asks, not moving.

I get up and light the stove, look out the window. You're stuck here for a few days, I say. I jerk my head out at the ice. Stranded, I say. If you need to use the phone to make some calls, go ahead. I'll leave you alone. And then I walk out of the cabin, sit out in the sun for about ten minutes. Just feel it on my face. Spreading slowly. When I go back into the cabin, he's still lying on the bed. Asleep again.

It's a small cabin for two people. He has nothing to do here. I can paint, but he's lost. He paces anxiously around the cabin for a whole day, watching me work. I'm sitting on a little fold-out stool, the kind you use for fishing, in front of my easel. I have the easel set higher than the chair, so that I'm generally always looking up at the canvas. I'm working on something sort of Braquian, for lack of a better term — a cubist construct with lots of browns and dull blues — and he stands behind me with his head tilted, watching.

Kind of like watching paint dry, I joke.

He laughs. Leans forward and puts his hands on my shoulders. He puts his mouth by my ear and asks softly, So where am I in all that?

I turn my head and look at him. Sorry?

Where am I, he says, waving his finger at the canvas, in all that?

I look at the canvas, raise my eyebrows. I sit back, stare at the painting. I don't know, I say, a little surprised.

What do you mean? he asks.

Well, I mean, it's abstract. It's not that deliberate. Or at least it's not apparent right away what things are. It's not that mapped out.

He nods, walks over to the armchair and sits in it. He stares out of the window for the rest of the evening. It's the end of March. It's finally staying light later. Till about 7:30 these days.

The next couple of days are grey. Low, misty cloud. The snow continues to melt, the ice starts thawing from the shore first, dissolving away from land. He's starting to go a little crazy. I know because he does the same things I do — taps his feet constantly while sitting, walks quickly in circles whenever he can, jumps up and down in the middle of the room just to burn energy. From my fold-out stool, just past the easel, I can see him outside in front of the cabin, muttering to himself, pacing. I watch him take a run at the icy water, and I stand up and knock the stool over as he stops himself, skipping, just before he gets to it.

I put down my paintbrush and go outside. Nathaniel, I say. He's staring at the water, turns when he hears his name. I go over and wrap my arms around him. He wraps his arms around me too, rests his cheek on the top of my head. You never say my name, he says. I hold him until I can feel him relax. Come on, I say. Let's get drunk.

All I have is bourbon — a good one too. I tell him that an old boyfriend, a flamenco-guitar player from Boston, of all places, introduced me to Maker's Mark years ago, and that to this day it's the only hard liquor I can drink.

Why do you think that is? he asks.

I don't know, I say. There was something about watching him drink it… He would put the glass to his lips, I say, smell it a bit before he sipped, close his eyes, tip the glass, and you could see a transformation. You could literally see warmth spread across his face. It was a very powerful thing. It was the only time I could talk to him, after he'd had his first drink. And before he had his third.

He nods. Like watching someone drink stars, he says.

*(Like watching someone drink stars.)*

I pour two drinks, two fingers each. If you want ice, I say, you'll have to go outside and chip your own. He shakes his head. Straight is fine, thanks.

I give him his glass. We hold them up to each other in a toast, and then it seems we both remember the story I just told, and become cautious, just for a moment.

I clink his glass. And we drink.

★

Two hours later, we're well on the way to drunk. It's still light out, and he's going on and on about how much fun it is to drink during the day. It's like seeing a matinee, he says. Absolute luxury.

The bottle's just about two-thirds full. I'm lying on the bed, on my back, my head just off the foot end, so that my head's tilted back and my hair's touching the floor. He's pulled the armchair up to the bed and is sitting in it with his bare feet drumming on my stomach. His head is resting against the back of the chair.

Have you noticed, I say, kind of slurry, that since we started talking, we've stopped having sex?

He rolls his head towards me. What?

We don't have sex anymore.

He laughs. What do you mean "anymore"? He takes a sip of bourbon.

Never mind.

Well, he says, you can't have both. I mean, it's either one or the other, right? he says, looking at me with half-closed eyes, his arm lolling off the armrest.

I close my eyes, feel the room start to spin. I hear him get out of the chair. I lift my head to put it flat on the bed. I feel the bed dip. I open my eyes halfway — he's on it, taking his shirt off. You want to paint me again? he asks. Huh? I laugh and shake my head. He straddles me, takes my arms and places them by my head. He puts one of my wrists on top of the other and then holds them down with his hand. He pushes down, hard. Huh? What do you want to do then?

I look at him. I'm quiet. Not scared. More like confused.

He lets go of my wrists, but I leave them there. He sits back on my thighs so I can't move under him. He unzips his pants, pulls out a half-erect penis. He leans forward, starts kissing me, sloppily, on the lips. I don't fight it, but I'm having a hard time kissing back. It's only the second time he's kissed me since he got here. Four days ago.

He sits back again, looks at his penis. It's the same, kind of bobbing, nodding downward. He sways, then puts his hands on the front of my jeans, starts to undo them. I keep my arms above my head, watching him. He gets all of the buttons undone, then tries to take my jeans off. I press my bum down on the bed to make it difficult. He struggles, not noticing what I'm doing, tries to work down one side at a time. Finally he stops, still straddling me, fully erect.

Stick out your tongue, he says. I do, slowly. He runs his palm over it. Then puts his palm over his penis, starts to rub it. Closes his eyes

## Ice Out

and rubs and rubs, groans like he does when I give him head. Except after a couple of minutes, he's only half as hard as he was.

He rolls his head around with closed eyes, then stops, looks at me. He straightens up on his knees, leans over, grabs the bottle of Maker's Mark that's on the floor by the bed. He opens it and sits back against my thighs, looks at me and slugs a mouthful back. Misses his mouth a little. Penis stiffening. Some of the bourbon drips onto it. He looks down, and slowly, very slowly, a smile creeps across his face. He holds out his hand, cups it. Pours a little bourbon into it. Puts the bottle next to his thigh. Wraps his bourbon-filled hand around himself. Starts to rub up and down. Erratically, because he's drunk. The smell of alcohol cuts the air between us.

I lie there, wide-eyed, watching. Stone sober all of a sudden, but feeling trapped, like I need to find that layer of air, press my lips against the layer that's keeping me under, so I can take a breath and inch my way back to the hole I came through.

He's rubbing so hard it looks painful. His eyes are squeezed shut, his tongue pressed up against the back of his bottom teeth. Holy Christ, I'm thinking, what is worth this? He's silent then, still rapidly pulling on himself, his hand slapping against his stomach. Looks down and again notices that he's half as hard as when he started out. Fuck it, he says, and stops. I swear I watch his penis deflate. I don't even want to blink. Don't want to miss a thing. A feeling of, once experiencing something, wanting to move back towards innocence. My heart beating like mad. Get him the fuck out of here.

My wife's going to kill me.

I shift a little, so I can look up at his face. What?

My wife, he says, slurring. She'll kill me if she ever finds out.

He grabs the bottle by his thigh, swings it up so that the bourbon makes a clinking sound in the glass almost. Takes a big swig. Brings the bottle down. Ah, he says, grins, lips and chin wet. He looks at me. Want some? I shake my head, slowly.

Your wife, I say. You mean your ex. He shakes his head slowly, sadly. And then he starts to cry.

★

In the morning, I get out of bed and trip over the bottle. I pick it up and put it on the counter. The bourbon inside splishes against the glass. There's just a bit left in it. Enough to soak a rag. I stand at the counter and drink two glasses of water. I fill the glass again and walk over to the window that faces the lake. I get the binoculars, try to see if there's a way through the ice yet. I scan the bay. None that I can see. Fuck.

He groans. I lean against the windowsill, look over at him on the bed. He tries to sit up. Holds his head in his hands. Oh, God, he says. Drink some water, I say.

He squints up at me, looks down, nods slightly. He's got four days of grey stubble now and his hair is greasy enough that it looks wet. It's kind of molded to the sides of his forehead, like Caesar. Except not as elegant. He looks ten years older than he is. Like Dylan after a revivalist road trip.

He gets up for a glass of water, looks at me while he gulps it. When he finishes, he brings the hand holding the empty glass up, wipes his mouth on the back of it. Points at the binoculars with the glass. You see anything? I keep looking at him and I shake my head.

I go over to my laundry pile, dig out some clothes. I take off the ones I'm wearing — still from the day before — and put the new ones on. He asks if there's any coffee. I shrug. Beans are on the counter, I say. You know the drill. I can feel him looking at me but I keep my back to him, pretending to fold my dirty clothes. I hear him open the tin of coffee beans and pour some into the grinder. He goes and sits in the armchair and starts grinding. I turn around.

He looks at me without saying anything.

I walk out of the cabin.

I go down to the boathouse, thinking I'll check the engine on the outboard. Now's as good a time as any. There's still some ice inside because the sun hasn't got to it, but it'll be gone in a couple of days. I flip the boat into slushy water, lift the engine off the dock, stagger into the boat with it and mount it on the back. I hook up the gas lines, choke it and pull on the ripcord a few times, but nothing happens. Just metallic, rambly coughs that die. He appears in the doorway. Need some help?

You do it, I say. My arms are too short. I swear these things are designed by people who are six feet tall. He steps down into the

## Ice Out

boat, pulls and gets it on the first try. There's lots of blue smoke, the engine rattly. He laughs at me. Says it's not because I'm a foot shorter than him. You're just not strong enough.

Fuck you, I'm stronger than you are, I say.

What, from holding a paintbrush all day?

Fuck you.

He starts laughing, not a nice laugh, a malicious one.

I can start the stupid engine, I say. It just takes me a few tries.

He reaches over, twists the throttle low, till it quits. Be my guest, he says.

I get in the boat, set the throttle on high, pull the choke, yank the cord. Nothing. Yank again. Nothing. I do this about ten times, till I can feel sweat breaking out on my forehead. Hair is falling over my face.

This is so fucking symbolic, I say.

What is?

This. Of what's happening. Of what this is.

Oh, is this some kind of artist's rhetoric now?

What if it is? I'm an artist. What difference does it make to you? It's my deal.

So what is this then? he asks.

Nothing. It's nothing.

No really, answer me.

I just did. It's nothing. I pause. So you tell me what this is then, I say.

I don't know what it is.

Yeah, you do. (I close my eyes.) What colour are my eyes?

What?

Yours are green. Henna, I say. What are mine?

This is stupid.

(I open them.)

Brown, he says, kind of surprised.

Cute, I say.

I thought henna was red, he says.

It's green before you add water, almost black when it's wet. Red when it dries. So take your pick. It's whatever you want it to be.

He smiles. As if to say *exactly*.

He gets up.

I grab his arm, hold him back.

He pushes my hand off him, gets into the boat, pulls the ripcord on the engine, and puts it in gear, cranking the throttle. The boat swoops upward, away from the dock in a straight line, wake like a veil. He's heading straight for the ice. I'm yelling at him to stop. It's not my boat. He'll hurt himself. I know he can't hear me, but I yell anyway. The whine of the engine softens. He lets go of the throttle. The boat dips down and forward in waves of backwash. He stands on the seat, looks towards me. I'm mad. My hands are clenched. I raise them and I shout, The only reason I know what colour your fucking eyes are is because I paint! He puts his hands in his pockets, looks out over the front of the boat towards the lodge. He turns back, steps down, swivels the engine so the boat swings towards the boathouse. He grabs the ripcord, then straightens up and looks at me. He shrugs, as if to say *Why the hell should I care?*, looks back at the engine, and pulls the cord. Gets it on the first try. Keeps the engine cranked so that the boat turns away again and starts heading for open water.

Granted, I've only been here for one spring so far, but I know that the direction he's heading is the wrong one. It's the last part of the lake that breaks up, except he can't see that from where he is. Big, solid ice. He'll hit it and go under in a second. I watch him dodge through the slush for a bit, shaking my head. I don't believe this. He's getting frustrated — I can see it in how he's turning the boat, fast one way, then back the other. Finally he goes full throttle and runs the thing up *onto* the ice. He cuts the engine and walks up to the bow of the boat. He steps off into ankle-deep water, onto ice, crouching to steady himself against the bow. It holds. He starts walking, carefully. Gets more confident the farther from the boat he gets. The ice under the bow of the boat cracks, sinks. The boat drifts slowly backward off the slab, spins slowly around to face me. He looks back and waves. I can see the white of his grin. "You fucker," I whisper. But it doesn't matter, does it, because he's gone. Not turning back. A chipmunk chatters beside me. The first chipmunk of the year. God, spring really is here. I look up at sun, feel it warm, really warm, on my face for the first time in six months. Now that's satisfying.

Someone, a happily married friend, told me once that fooling around with other women made him feel less exposed and less vulnerable to his wife. To commit to someone, he said, is to brush away a sort of topsoil that covers your life. And to ask them to brush away theirs. When you commit to someone, he said, you're not who you were without them. You and the other person create ephemeral third and fourth people, who have elements of both of you, but who would never exist independently of you. And the person you thought was yourself is suddenly gone. Which is, he seems to think, why affairs happen.

I walk behind the boathouse, pull back a tarp that's still got a bit of clear, sugary snow on it. I tip a cedar-strip canoe away from the wall, drag it down onto the dock. Go into the boathouse and get a paddle and some rope.

By the time I've reached the boat, he's reached shore. I watch him disappear into some bushes and see him emerge on the lawn of the lodge a couple of minutes later. Watch him walk diagonally up it, small and out of focus, hunched over like that famous picture of the Yeti running up a mountainside, scared of having been discovered, running from the risk of exposure. I tie the boat to the stern of the canoe and paddle back to the boathouse. Zig-zagging away from him.

A couple of days later, he calls me from his cell to tell me to be sure to turn my clocks forward that night. Daylight Savings. That's all he calls to say. I want to tell him that I don't have any clocks to set forward (remember?), but thanks anyway. I want to tell him that I heard the first summer loon call today, that one, you know, the long *whoooooo-eeeeeee-oooo* that sends shivers down every Canadian's spine. I want to tell him that ice out is almost over, that I can get from the cabin to the lodge with the canoe now, but he hangs up before I say anything.

# Etching

I STAND IN FRONT of a red Honda Civic with Quebec plates. Its windshield is caved, but not so smashed that you can't see the blood and hair stuck to it on the underside. In two places, about four feet apart, driver, passenger. It's at an auto wreckers on the outskirts of Calgary, and the car's about two years newer than the one my father used to own. When I first started doing this it took me a while to see the pattern — that I was always drawn to the types of cars that close friends and family owned. It used to worry me that I wasn't being objective. Now I just let it happen. Tell myself it's as random as anything.

It's not so much the physical smashed-upness of the car or how it happened that I'm interested in. What I'm interested in is far more personal. Perverse, even, to some. I'm interested in what's *inside* the car. In who was injured, or who died. In what was taken.

In the Honda cassette tapes are strewn everywhere. k.d. lang. Dead Can Dance. An old, original *Songs of Kris Kristofferson*. "Me and Bobby McGee." "You Show Me Yours (And I'll Show You Mine)." *Loving her was easier than anything I'll ever do again.* I walk around the car and think about that line for a moment, wonder if Kristofferson thought that was true when he sang it, or if it was just something that sounded real good.

The front driver's-side wheel is crunched at an angle of forty-five degrees up into the wheel well. Tire flat. Looks like they got hit from the front, and maybe a bit from the side. Definitely by something much bigger than the car.

My cellphone rings. It's you, your sweet voice. I lean against the car and peer into the driver's-side window, phone to my ear. You ask me what I'm up to. Inspecting tragedy, I say.

Something only a bachelor would do, you say, then ask: Internally or externally?

I consider that for a while. Ostensibly externally, I say. I shade my hand over my eyes, look around. Not much in the front seats. A Slurpee cup. Tim Hortons wrappers. A book. I tell you I'm at a wrecking yard, standing beside a '93 Civic, Quebec plates, fair amount of blood. I walk around to the back, stick my hand in through the windowless hatchback. Finger some clothes. A Walkman. Not much else. I open the passenger-side door. Reach between the seats. Pick up the book. A road atlas. *Bon mariage! Bonne chance!! Bon voyage!!!* written on it. Newlyweds. Oh, God, I say.

They'd drawn their route so far. Started just under the curl of the Gaspé. Crossed over at Trois-Rivières, then up through Cochrane, Kap, Sioux Lookout, (page over) Winnipeg, Yorkton, Saskatoon. Stopped drawing at Chinook. Just this side of the border.

You tell me you have something you want to talk to me about. A proposal. A collaboration. I stop flipping through the atlas. I think, swallow. Say sure.

You ask where I am, say you'll come pick me up. I tell you that I'm at Portland and Blackfoot, but that I can find my way to your place. You insist, say you're at your studio, which is close by.

Give me another twenty minutes or so, I say. I take this ritual of mine seriously. I still need to talk to the guy who owns the wreckers and ask him what he knows about the people who were inside the car.

Which I do. And when he tells me they were cut off by the back end of an eighteen-wheeler, that they'd both been killed when they'd collided with the concrete barrier, I ask him if I can keep the atlas, and a tape. He looks at me strange, then shrugs and says Sure, why not. But I know he won't look me in the eye again or wave at me when I leave. It's the same at all these places. The people running these yards don't understand the concept or nobility of salvage beyond the physical. They just want to sell you that one hubcap you're missing from your Taurus, or a distributor cap for your kid's beater. They don't get atlases and tapes. They don't get the humanity that underlies what they do.

You show up after half an hour. I raise a palm to the owner of the yard, who turns his head in the other direction, doesn't wave back. I

*Etching*

get into your car, sit back in the seat, look out the side window. You don't ask any questions. At the first stoplight, I lean forward and put the tape into your stereo.

I look around your car, wonder what I'd find if I saw it at a wreckers. Funny, I never noticed what kind it was before. I ask if it's a Chrysler.

You scoff. It's a Lexus.

I apologize. Pretty shiny stuff for an artist, I say.

It's Jerry's, you say, and I nod. That explains it.

There's not much lying around. No errant mail or invitations to openings with your name on them wedged into the front of the passenger-side footspace, or mint wrappers or receipts from Harry Rosen or the lunches on Jerry's expense account. Just Jerry's stainless-steel travel mug sitting neatly in its holder, looking like it's never had anything in it. I ask you how long he's owned the car.

Four years, you say. It still smells brand new. Leather seats. I grip the edges of mine, feel a certain smoothness seeping into me, one that comes with owning a car like this, a smoothness that I'm incapable of.

The music plays, a little warped at first. You belt out *Busted flat in Baton Rouge, headin' for the train…*

When I was a kid, I say, we used to listen to this album a lot. We were listening to it one day, a Saturday, I think, and at the end of it my mom said *He was a Rhodes Scholar, you know*. I didn't know what that meant, heard "road scholar" and thought that was the coolest thing in the world you could be. A few years later, I read the back of the album where it spells out the academic career he abandoned for song-singing — the place where it said "Rhodes Scholar" — and I felt unhappy about that. For the longest time, I say, I had an idea of Kristofferson being a hitchhikin', train-jumpin' wanderer. And still try to.

You say that your dad used to sing this song when he was drunk. Back when it first came out.

I ask if he still sings it. You shake your head, tell me that the more desperate his life gets, the more he prefers melodrama. I laugh, and ask if he listens to Edith Piaf, or something. Close, you say. He only sings arias from tragic operas now. Songs of impending doom.

After a moment of silence, you start to tell me your proposal.

You tell me about the process of deconstructing a photograph. You enlarge it again and again on a photocopier, you say, using the previous photocopy each time. It used to be a lot easier, when photocopiers were shitty. Now you have to do it, like, a hundred times. That's what we should do with your sculpture, you say. You know, the one with all the salad forks you stole from the Palliser? Photograph it with a Polaroid and then enlarge it until it falls apart.

On the page, you mean.

Yes. Then make a plate and print it.

I smile. OK.

★

Your studio's basically a tin shack in between an industrial park and a field. The rent's so cheap you're practically squatting. We're sitting on milk crates in the first sun of spring, out back behind it, taking a break from looking at the photocopies, talking about love.

You ask me why I followed my last girlfriend to Europe and it seems like a bad time to admit to you that I've ever failed at anything so I put a pathetic, noble spin on it. I say that I went because masochism can be educational; that when you break up with someone in a long and drawn-out way (in Vienna, in Prague, and again, finally, in Geneva) you learn more about yourself, instead of saying *fuck you, I'm better than this* and leaving.

You're quiet. You take a drag on your cigarette, pull your jacket tighter around you. We sit in silence for about five minutes. Watch the wind twist through the wheat in front of us.

You look down at one of the photocopies, run your finger over an arc of black grainy spots where a tine used to be. You tilt your head, look at it from a different angle.

Well, should we get back to it? you say.

And I nod.

I take the photocopy from you and look at it. Neither of us is really sure what the piece will be, but you've assured me that deconstructing a physical form with a combination of technology and ancient printing methods will be poignant. I forget why.

Jerry doesn't get it, you say, but I've given up trying to explain it to him.

*Etching*

I could try, I say, if you want.
Nah, that's OK, you say. He'll never understand what I'm doing.
Is that a problem?
Sometimes, you say.
Do you understand what he does?
Nope.
What does he do?
Banking.
Yeah, but what, specifically?
That's all we need to know, you say, according to him.
Hmmmm, I say. But at least you balance each other out.
You just look at me.
Yes, well, then there's Geneva, I say. Just an ocean away.
Let's work, you say.

★

I'm at your house. Jerry's barbecuing some steaks. The first barbecue of the year. Your parents are on their way over and you and I are digging in the basement for all the summer eating stuff. Paper plates. Plastic cutlery. Paper napkins your mother bought for you at the MOMA in New York, from a trip they took after the attacks just to show their patriotism. The napkins have Warhol soup cans on them: your mother's attempt at understanding you as an artist. She doesn't know you hate Warhol. They didn't even go into the museum, you say. They just stopped in at the shop. You let out a malicious chuckle and shake your head. The closest they ever come to art is moulding consumption into a form of it, you say. A smile breaks across your face and you say Let's use all the napkins tonight. You make me promise to take and discard at least one for each course, then pause to enjoy the significance of destroying them in an ostentatious fashion.

I've never met your father so I ask you about him, ask you what he's like.

You just stand there for a moment. Then you shake your head.

I see some plastic cups buried behind a box. I hand it to you, pull the cups out and turn to take the box from you again. But you're standing there with it in your hands, staring at it.

It's a small box. An old cigar box, though you told me no one in your family ever smoked, which is why you don't mind the occasional cigarette. You like the smell right after one's been lit, you told me a while ago. After that, it becomes offensive.

You open the box. Your eyes widen, then get sad. You frown, hand the box to me with the lid open.

There's a child's ring with Babar the Elephant's wife — was it Celeste? — on it, the kind of ring you'd imagine falling out of a box of sugary cereal and into your bowl.

There's a gimp bracelet. Blue and green. I made this at camp, you say, picking it up, trying it on. It still fits.

There's one of those folded puzzles you put on the tips of your fingers for answers to the urgent questions you have when you're ten years old — something where you choose a number and a colour and you spell them out as you spread your fingers back and forth. A paper fortune teller, the answers revealed under flaps in between your fingers. *Orange. Eight. Yes, he loves you.*

A couple of varsity letters. I raise my eyebrows. For what? I ask. Tennis, you say, taking them and closing the box. Embarrassed.

I saw a movie the other day where a man engaging in compulsive thievery says that everyone has a box of stuff they hide so it can be found by someone else. Knowing someone else has seen it merely helps the owner realize who they are, the thief says, as he's taking someone's box. *You take it away and show them what they had.*

I put the box back. We go upstairs. Your parents have arrived. We were digging out summer stuff, I say. You wave the napkins at your mother. Her face falls. You still have those? she asks, taking them. Oh my, she says, running a hand over them. Oh yes. I remember that trip very well. As though it were a hundred years ago.

We found shocking evidence of Pauline's past, I say to your father.

What's that? he says, all them freaky drawings she did as a kid?

No, I say, a little taken aback. Her varsity letters.

He looks at me like I'm nuts.

Tennis, I say.

He squints an eye at me.

She was Alberta High School Champion, Dear, your mother says to him, but he's already turning toward the barbecue, flicking his eyes up, looking away.

## Etching

While we eat, your father talks about shootin' coon and how you fucked up your life and when I start to defend you, you wave your hand at him, look at me and say Honey on a rock, Neil. Jerry looks at me and nods once, head tilting to the side. Like he's tried a million times already. I can believe that. Jerry's a good guy.

You sit down in front of your father and tell him you're going to read a poem you've written about him. He squirms and you smile and Jerry touches your arm as you get up. You read the poem (a good one) and I watch your father's face soften when you start to read; there's a tenderness in his eyes it's obvious he'd hate to admit to. It makes me think he's terrified of displayed emotion and that your reading's not so that you can see his tenderness (because it's way too late for that to matter), but so that you can say *fuck you* in a way that neither of you objects to, though your father starts to hum *Un di felice* from *La Traviata* before you finish. Your mother worries her napkin (and then yours) into corkscrews of pulp. She starts to cry and your father says Oh for God's sake Margaret, they're just words. They don't mean a damn thing.

★

There are several stages involved in making an etching plate — you start with a blank copper sheet and coat it in wax. You etch lines into the wax, then soak the plate in a bath of acid. You use Varsol to remove the wax and the image on the plate blooms. Any part of the plate which has had wax on it remains untouched by the acid. Pristine. You keep dipping the plate in wax, then etch more lines and dip it in acid, each time eating away at the plate a little more so that you move from having one which produces definitive lines — straight black-and-white images — to a plate with complex shading. You have to do it in stages because you'll never get it right on the first one. You have to keep testing to see how far along you are, to see if things are working.

The plate is done. You take some aquatint crystals, scrape and stir them into a thick, syrupy ink. You take a card and stack the ink against it, then smear it over the plate, sweeping smoothly. You make sure you get all the lines inked, make sure the whole plate is covered, that the ink has really sunk into the lines you've etched. The sound of thick cardboard scraping on copper takes over the room. You wipe the surface of the plate clean.

★

The next day on the drive back from the studio, you say Let's get some ice cream. I've got a special place where we can eat it.

You make an awkward, one-handed turn off the highway, holding the cone in your other hand, chocolate trailing down your wrist. I offer to hold the cone for you, but you shake your head. We drive down a dirt road for a few hundred metres, its edge blurred by a collision of mushrooming dust and arching alder. We stop on a small bridge — a new one made of white concrete barriers. You laugh and point to a long line of basketball-sized marijuana leaves that have been spray-painted evenly along it as though masquerading as oversized rivets. School just got out and the kids are already bored, you say. You run your tongue up your forearm, erasing the track of ice cream. Mmmmm, you say. Come on. I know where we can find some shade.

We get out of the car and walk to the edge of the bridge. We hear some splashing and when we come down along a path that goes under the bridge we come across a couple of twelve-year-olds wading in the creek. It hasn't rained in a while, so the creek's pretty low, but it's hot enough that just looking at water makes things seem cooler.

We sit on a rock under the bridge, eat ice cream. Licking. Chocolate. Rum 'n' Raisin. I almost tell you that I haven't had Rum 'n' Raisin for about twenty years, but suddenly that seems like a drab detail, so I just sit there and stare at the kids. Take a bite.

One of the kids is chubby, his wet T-shirt clinging to the rolls of his belly when he stands — goofy, but cute. He sloshes over to the edge of the creek, a rocky part, where the water's knee-deep. He lies bellydown and I imagine his stomach touching the bottom, grazing shale.

The other kid follows him over. He's slim, striking, so goodlooking you'd expect him to be making fun of the other one, like in some Stephen King story set in the '50s. To be calling him names. *Phat boy. Chubby Chicken. Lard ass.* But he doesn't. Which, it occurs to me, might be why they're under a bridge on a creek that runs

## Etching

away from the highway, a few kilometres from town. I look over at you. You're watching them. You've stopped licking your ice cream.

The cute kid is standing over the chubby one. The chubby one's looking up at him, laughing. The cute one leans a little further down, laughs back. He lifts his foot and places it on a rock on the other side of the chubby kid, straddling him. Neither one stops looking at the other. The cute one leans down some more.

Wow, I say.

The kids snap their heads over towards us. They stare at us for a moment, and all we can hear is the creek trickling. A dragonfly buzzing between us. You shift on the rock. The kids look back at each other and the chubby one smiles, turns slowly onto his stomach.

You look at me. Yes. You say. Wow.

We climb back onto the bridge and sit with our legs dangling off it, watching the water flow slowly over rocks. One of the boys' laughs echoes off the underside of the bridge, floats up past our feet. Another one follows. A red ribbon is caught on some weeds under the surface of the creek and we watch it pulse back and forth with the current. Sway underwater.

Back on the highway, I've got my window rolled down, my hand on the side mirror, the wind pushing through the sleeve of my T-shirt. Green fields rushing past. I ask you if you think your father had a good time last night.

You smile, watch the road. I don't know, you say. After a few minutes, you ask me if you ever told me about the helicopter dad. No, I say.

There was a series of letters on the Internet a while ago, written by this guy who fights fires from helicopters, you say, and they were so beautiful.

You tell me that this guy, who's in his mid-fifties, is visiting his twenty-five-year-old daughter in New York City one day. She works in a bookstore and is showing him around. He has an epiphany while he's in the store, you say, realizes that he has no idea his *daughter* had to know so much to sell books, to *be who she was* and where did she learn that kind of stuff? So when he goes home he starts to write her these really long letters telling her all about what *he* does, telling her the specifics of his job, telling her where he learned all *his* kind of stuff, telling her all these things about him that she'd never guess — that he flew a bunch of Donald Trump's helicopters from New Jersey to Alaska once, all painted black with solid-gold fixtures inside, knowing they were going to be gutted and used by the forest service — those kinds of details. The kinds of details you'd think you wouldn't be interested in, but which you suddenly are because he's discovering his daughter as a person and he's surprised by it, wants to make use of it after years of thinking he knew all there was to know about her just because he was her father. And that she knew everything about him just because she was his daughter. He keeps writing these letters, you say, and she keeps posting them on the Internet. And you keep reading them.

You're quiet for a few minutes. Green fields rushing past. Wind pushing up my sleeve. So after I read the first few, you say, I wrote my dad a letter.

I raise my eyebrows. And?

And it was the same kind of letter — one where I told him why I'm an artist, why I chose mixed media, gave him small details that I thought would make him see that he loved me or that even if he didn't, he was wrong to resent me. I gave up trying to understand him a long time ago, because it prevented me from doing my work.

I'm silent.

I wrote to him, you say, that when a piece really comes together, there's no feeling anywhere else in the world like that. That it's a difficult place to get to, but when you get there you feel as though anything is possible. I told him that getting to the core of a piece must be what having a child is like. All probability and obstacle. But the euphoria in it can be mind-blowing. If you let it.

And?

And nothing, you say. You stare at the road. Are quiet until the turnoff. And he never wrote one back, you say.

Oh, I say. I reach out to put my hand on your shoulder but stop before I get there. I'm sorry, but did you really expect him to?

I guess not, you say. The thing is, he and I get along best when we don't say anything at all. And that bothers me.

We pull into your driveway. Jerry's standing at the end of it, a dirty shovel in his hand. He stays there and looks at us. Expressionless.

Are you and Jerry going to have kids? I ask.

No, you say.

## Etching

I look at him and then back at you. Everything OK? I ask.

Oh yeah, you say. I think so. (You pause.) Oh, it's not what you're thinking… Jerry would never screw around. He's not capable of it.

That wasn't what I was thinking, but I don't say that.

There's a picture of you and of him in the hallway of your house. He's sitting directly behind you, has his arm wrapped all the way around you. And your smiles are so genuine that every time I see it I wonder why I'm so incapable of something normal, why everything that I consider good for myself has to be dramatic. I want to tell you that when I saw that picture the first time, I wondered if I'd ever loved anyone at all. But then I remember that I dismissed the thought immediately. Geneva. Vienna. Prague.

We're going to the lake for a barbecue on Canada Day, you say. Come with us.

★

Each print needs to be inked separately, you say. I hand you a sheet of paper and you lay it on top of the plate, cover it with a big felt blanket to protect it from the pressure of the roller.

While we work you tell me that you lived across from a church once. It was when I didn't have a studio, you say, so I worked at home. And one day I was so utterly fed up with the piece I was working on — you look up at me — you know the one with the stencil of Stalin? (I nod.) That one, you say. The glue drove me nuts. Anyway, I was about to slash the whole thing with a box cutter when I looked out the window and saw this big white limo pull up to the church.

You crank the handle and move the roller slowly across the plate. My fingers are running over the felt, smoothing it before the roller hits. *Not necessary to the process, but it makes a better print.*

A groom and all his groomsmen stepped out, you say. Other people started to arrive. And I said fuck it and had a shower and threw on the only dress I had that wasn't black and crashed the wedding.

You're not supposed to wear black at a wedding?

No, you say. It's bad luck.

You peel back the felt and pull the sheet away from the plate, look at the print. You have to understand that this was in a pretty rough part of town, you say. Not a lot of people choosing to get married there. Plus, the church was for sale.

You're kidding.

No. I mean, God. Isn't that portentous? To have a *For Sale* sign on the church you're getting married in? And in the photos? The thing had plywood doors, for Christ's sake. I always felt like weddings there weren't going to be marriages that worked out. That, and other things...

Like? I take the print from you, put it on a drying rack by the door.

Like... the bride arriving before everyone else — too anxious. And using a limo company whose name begins with three As. Aaardvark Limo Services.

Aardvark only has two As.

This one had three. And people still used them.

You went to more than one wedding?

Yes.

Weren't they all the same?

Yes. Except for one.

Your arms are getting tired. There's four tons of force per square inch on that paper when it goes under the roller, you told me last week. You let me take one of the spokes of the handle and you stand behind me, putting your hands on top of mine. You push the roller over the paper with me. There, you say, you feel the impression? Your hands are warm. The stone of your wedding ring has flipped to the inside of your hand and cuts into my ring finger. Tell me about that wedding, I say.

The bride had a fabulous dress. Made of bubble wrap. (I laugh.) And they told me that they couldn't afford to get married in a big, regular church, so originally they wanted to get married in an inflatable one their friend had made with only enough room for them, the priest and two witnesses, down at her parents' farm near Pincher Creek, but it was too windy there for that so they settled for a church in the city that was for sale.

And? I ask.

And I always thought that one would work out.

Hmmm, I say.

And you? you ask.

## Etching

Me what?

What do you think?

I don't know, I say. I pick up one of the prints and look at it. Lines and dots that used to be arcs and thin beams. That used to be a photograph of something that was six feet tall and made with spindles of steel.

I have this friend who was with a woman for seven years once, I say. Not the kind of guy you could ever picture married. And sure enough, he was happy not being married to her, but one weekend he got pressured into it by her brother. They were all in Calgary and they got drunk and the brother basically nailed him up against a brick wall in the back alley of Cowboys and said *You fucker, if you don't marry my sister I'll beat the living crap out of you.* So that was that. They got married the next day. He bought a seersucker suit and they went to the Justice of the Peace down the street and they got married. And on the way back, he changed in the back of the car and returned the suit. I always liked the raw honesty of that, I say. Of returning the suit.

You stop and blink hard, staring at me.

I look up at you. Don't get me wrong. It's not something I'd ever do — I just like that someone else did it. That bubble wrap dress — it's the same thing. It's putting that fear on display.

And? you ask.

And they got divorced a year later. He said things changed after they got married. I always wanted to ask him if maybe they hadn't; if maybe the differences that led to their divorce had always been there but had been ignored — pockets of delusion, none of them connecting, like bubble wrap. And if once they tied the knot there was simply no easy way out.

You have an issue with fidelity, you say.

I tell you that I don't see how it affects me the way it affects others, that I've never been prone to romance of the suburban-housing kind, but, as best as I can figure, I want fidelity, think it's noble, just can't seem to find it.

You look at me and instead of shifting your eyes away like you normally do you hold your gaze for about half a minute. You open your mouth to say something, then change your mind. Close it. Look away.

And? I say.

You pull the last sheet out from under the roller. *And*, you say, I think that wondering whether all those marriages would work out never stopped me from getting married. In a field. With wildflowers growing all around us.

No church, I say.

No church.

You laugh. You've got ink on your face, you say. And instead of showing me on your own face where the ink is, you reach out and gently touch where it is on mine. You hesitate first, then run a shaky fingertip along my chin. Here, you say. Stop and raise your finger to a spot on my cheek. And here.

You look at me as though you're wondering if I mind that you're doing this. I haven't felt bashful, like I couldn't touch someone without becoming embarrassed, in years. I want to hold your face in both of my hands.

I want to show you something, you say. You pull me outside, lock the studio and lead me to the field behind it. We push our way through chest-high straw, wildflowers. After a few hundred feet, you stop and point. See?

I don't. But I'm shorter than you. You look back at me and a smile creeps slowly across your face. You say Don't worry, you will soon enough.

We continue to walk through the field. You stop and show me a flower. Bergamot, you say.

Really. I always thought bergamot grew in exotic places, I say. You pinch off a leaf from its stem, hold it out to me and tell me to eat it.

I put it in my mouth and close my eyes. It is. Exotic. Like heat that never dissipates at night.

I open my eyes and all I can see is your head. You're way ahead in the grass and the more you disappear, the more I can see what we're walking towards: a large, skeletal sculpture. Steel-beam skyscraper scaffolding that's been hammered into a shape that reminds me of a prehistoric creature: Brontosaurus, maybe. The one with all the spikes running down its back.

I'd totally forgotten about this, I hear you shout, until today.

You're completely gone. All I can see is the grass waving in front of you as you push it away.

*Etching*

★

On the drive home, you recite a poem, a beautiful one. Full of your favourite phrases, you say. Green fields rushing past.

*bright stain on her skin,*
Starting to yellow.
*fingertips a row of*
*small wounds*
Wind pushing up my sleeve.
*sadness that follows*
*the body's blind wanting,*

I look at you while you're reciting the poem
*There's that pit at the core*
*of sweetness*
and think this would be a good moment to die. Right now.

★

We go to the lake for Canada Day. Have the barbecue and stay until just after the fireworks start. Driving west, back to Calgary, we're catching up with the fading daylight. Eleven o'clock and still summer light low across the sky. Driving on a plain that stretches a thousand miles north, south, east. Every direction except west. You and Jerry in the front of the Lexus. Me in the rear, arm stretched across the top of the seat, looking back at where we came from.

The corn is low enough that you can still see the horizon, and gradually, like a hairy mould blooming, it becomes pocked with miniscule fountains of fireworks — silent, random, bursting then drooping in a blackening sky. Two hundred and seventy degrees of towns in the distance, celebrating.

In front of us, the explosions are obscured by land rising and falling, light like blitzkrieg bombing peppering towns to the west. A David Gray song playing on the radio so softly I crane to hear the words.

*skies*      *wild above*

*howl*      *face*

*everything*      *held*

*appear*      *trace*

La la la. Di da.

There are fireflies all around us, but I can only see them if I look out the side window. They turn invisible in front of us, and behind us.

I shiver.

Jerry reaches for your hand. You let him take it.

★

The day after Canada Day. You drop me off at my place and I tell you to come in, have a look at the next piece I'm working on. Composed entirely of things that belong to people who no longer exist, I say. You raise your eyebrows, grin, and are out of the car in a shot.

You spend about half an hour walking around it, asking questions. *What's this? Where did you find this guy's passport? Did this part surprise you?* A cock ring. Outside a police station. Yes.

Jerry's away, you say, trailing your finger on the edge of the piece.

And? I ask.

And I'm hungry. Do you have some tomatoes?

I open a bottle of wine and sit on the other side of my counter watching you. You tell me to put some pasta on while you throw some chopped tomatoes and garlic into a pan, add a splash of wine directly from your glass. You take an orange from a bowl of fruit on top of the fridge and cut a piece of skin so thin it's translucent. Into the pan. A bit of salt, the rest of your wine. You look at me to see my reaction because you know the wine is an expensive one, and when you see what you want — my brief look of shock and annoyance — you laugh, reach for my glass. I stare at you and let you take it. You stare back, smiling, take a long sip from it. Hand it back almost empty.

## Etching

You let the sauce simmer and refill our glasses. You ask if I have any sugar. I don't think so, I say, but will honey do?

Yes.

I come around the counter to get it. Reach high up into a cupboard while you say that you're always suspicious of people who keep honey and sugar out of reach. I hand you the jar with a look that says *just finish the damn sauce*. You lift the lid off the saucepan, look around for a spoon, can't find one. So you dip your finger into the honey, hold it over the pan, let it fall in a thin string that folds on top of itself in ribbons and dissolves. I watch you. Ask if that's the secret. You shrug, say that your grandmother always told you to add a pinch of sugar to something savoury, and a pinch of salt to anything sweet. Like sliced apples. She said it brought out all the flavour.

Your finger is coated in honey. You bring it towards your mouth, then change your mind, turn and hold it out for me to lick. I look at you, lean slowly towards you, wrap my mouth around your whole finger. I leave it there for a second, close my eyes and pull my mouth along it. Your finger is clean. You watch me as I roll my tongue around inside my mouth. I had a South Asian girlfriend once who said that food tastes better when mixed with the oil that comes off your skin. She was right. I've had this honey before, straight from a spoon, and it did not taste like this. You reach for my face, hold it in both of your hands, and kiss me. The honey has collected in the middle groove of my tongue, and we kiss until it's all gone.

It didn't feel like anything. Nothing. Not a thing. I told myself it was because you'd taken me by surprise.

★

The next night you and Jerry and I are at a party. Some fundraiser for a technology program at SAIT, very white, very friendly, very hands-off, in that naïve Calgary sort of way of extracting money from those who have it. *Place your cheques in this here box — we won't announce the amount.*

We're standing there and you start talking about the watercolour classes you're taking. You talk about your new instructor and how he's getting you used to spreading colour across the page, how liberating it is, but how you suddenly feel jarred from the foundation of your life. Jerry looks at you but doesn't say anything. Two beats. I'm going to get a drink, he says.

I watch him moving away from us in the crowd, his head disappearing behind a group of overweight men standing in a semi-circle with vodka tonics in their hands. I ask you if you want another drink and you nod your head. I make my way over to the bar. I get a glass of red wine, and a Caesar for you. As I'm paying, a woman comes up and asks the bartender if he has a cigarette. He nods and hands her one, flicks up the flame from a lighter.

I hate lighting these things, she says.

I'll do it, I say, reaching out for the cigarette, if you don't mind.

Not at all, she says. I light it and take two quick drags. I hand it back to her when it starts to burn sour and she says Thanks and walks away. The bartender looks at me and shrugs. I pick up the drinks and look to my right, and there's Jerry, talking to the woman. She looks at me, then smiles slightly, which makes Jerry turn around. I walk over to them. He looks me straight in the eye for a moment, as if trying to determine my motive, and when he sees that I have none, says to her, This is Neil.

Then he smiles. So does she. In a smirky kind of way. We smile at each other and no one says anything. I just stand there, taking them in while big oil men make deals and you stand alone, waiting, a hundred feet behind us. And I understand then that this woman in front of me, this woman with Jerry, is married, that she has a son or a daughter, maybe two, even, and that she isn't planning on leaving her husband. She takes a drag on her cigarette.

At that point, Jerry and the woman and I are all looking at each other, back and forth, and I start to laugh. He joins in and so does she, and it's a full, belly-clutching laugh, not an ounce of maliciousness in it whatsoever, and we laugh and laugh so much that everyone around us stops talking, stares at us and the infection spreads and they start to laugh too. Not even knowing why. But it feels like we're all in on it. That everything is OK.

I dab my eyes once on my sleeve, hoist my glass at Jerry and the woman, and they bring theirs together in a clink that resonates so deeply I know I'll remember it for months. Years, maybe. And I think then that marriage must be an emotional state, not a physical one, if everything's going to work out or survive a reinterpretation. That in marriage you have more room for wonder. When you're in a less committed relationship you're always worried about it ending. I read somewhere once that sometimes staying unmarried to someone is a greater infidelity than an affair. I turn and look at you, staring off in another direction thinking about watercolour, and I think it could be true.

I walk back over to you, rich smoke flavour still in my mouth, hand you your Caesar. You start talking right away about vermillion and its power to elevate dimension, or diminish it. How it harbours contradictory qualities.

Sometimes there's a moment of honesty within delusion that forces you to consider the consequences of being honest. I look back over at Jerry. He's telling the woman something, leaning into her as though the noise in the room is too loud for her to be able to hear him (it's not). I can see them smiling. The air between us crystal clear.

★

There's a truck, a red one, in the distance, speeding toward us along a dirt road, spitting up dust behind it. It drives and it drives and then it disappears behind a cornfield. Openness met with doom. An extreme confidence that no one will be approaching in just the same manner from either direction on the side roads that intersect it. A trust that there will be no collision, when it seems almost certain that there will. Part of me wants to imagine it, wants to be there when it happens, despite the damage witnessing it would do.

I tell you an old Persian (or is it Mexican?) adage. *The corn is high. There will be many children in nine months.* You like that, you get it. Most North Americans don't get it, I say, because we have plenty of privacy, can't imagine having to go into a cornfield to make love. Or having to wait till the corn is high enough to shed the fear of being discovered.

The smell of clover fills the car and you start to cry.

I put my hand on your shoulder and keep it there, feel your muscles move under it as you steer the car past the road that leads to the bridge with marijuana leaves on it.

There's a U2 cassette in the player, appropriated from a crumpled Cherokee.

*Baby please,*
*Baby don't bite your lip*
*Give you half what I got*
*If you untie the knot,*
*It's a promise.*

★

You want to deconstruct the etching further. Enlarge the etching of the endlessly photocopied picture of the sculpture until the collapsed image collapses, becomes not even a series of dots. Until it becomes something else. Then make it a lithograph. A blur of shades.

How about manipulating a photograph of your own, I want to say. The one in the hallway. I say I don't see the point.

You're letting your ego get in the way, you say. You don't want to do it because you can't see your work in it anymore.

But you could have done this with anything, I say.

You don't answer.

It's no longer artistic, I say. The technology has taken over.

That's the whole point, you say.

It's too convenient a point for me, I say.

Your face tightens. You press your lips together so hard they turn white. So now what?

And then suddenly, it's all clear. If you ask me, I say, I think you need to stop being so destructive.

You look at me.

You're trying to force an epiphany, I say, but all you wind up with — I point to the etching — is a mass of grey. Which is fine, if that's what it originally was, if your point is to create something solely through intervention. Your logic — if I understand it correctly — is to destroy something with the hope that you'll be reminded that you still believe in it. But in the process, you're still destroying it. You can't change that.

Get out, you say.

Sometimes you just have to be happy with the original, or with the grey, I say. Don't keep fucking with it. It's interesting as an idea, but it's non-executable, if you want anything to survive.

GET OUT, you shout.

*Etching*

★

*Baby please,*
*Baby please slow down*
*Baby I feel sick*
*Don't make me stick*
*To a promise.*

★

I call your house the following Sunday to see if I can go to your studio to pick up my stuff. Jerry answers, says he's thinking of trying to convince you to go to the lake to spend some time together. So it's probably a good time for you to go, he says.

OK, I say.

Hey Neil, he says.

Yeah?

I'm sorry things didn't work out.

It's for the best, I say. But thanks.

You take care.

Uh huh.

I used to think that silence was more of a betrayal than the honesty of outright betrayal. But now I realize that silence is just an acknowledgement of things that aren't so sharply defined, that giving confusion airtime might tip the precarious balance of love, tossing one person off it. So you stay quiet and everything goes back to normal, eventually. The teeter-totter balances itself.

So. I go to the studio in the early afternoon. Start clearing out my things. Wonder if I should take the plate to prevent you from doing anything with it. But then I realize I really don't care.

Your laugh outside the door. I look up. The handle turns and the door opens.

A man walks in, a bottle of champagne in his hand, you behind him. You see me, and your smile flashes to a stern line on your face. The man drops your hand, shoves his own into his pocket. Your fingers go up to your blouse, and you do up the button above your breasts without looking down. Run a hand through your hair and wipe the sweat that has suddenly sprung up on your nose.

I'm sorry, I say. Jerry said he and you were going to the lake.

We are, you say, just later on.

Oh, I say. And we stand there for a while in silence. The two of you stay in the doorway and I stand where I am, unable to move past you, to leave. All of us looking back and forth at each other.

Finally you say, Well, have a good weekend then, and back out of the doorway. OK, you too, I say, and the man shuts the door and I hear both of you walking away in silence. The car starts and I hear Kristofferson creep out from it. Windshield wipers slappin' time.

I look at the things I've gathered from your studio. Sit down at one of your tables and just stare at them for a while. In the corner I see the box that we found in your basement. I go over to it, run my fingers over one of the varsity letters. I put it down and pick up the paper-triangle finger game. I put it on the tips of my fingers.

*Pick a colour.*

Red.

I flick my fingers forward and to the side. R-E-D.

*Pick a number between one and ten.*

One-two-three-four. Look inside for the answer.

*Yes, he loves you.*

*Pick another colour.*

B-L-U-E.

*Pick a number between one and ten.*

One-two-three-four-five-six-seven times. Look at the answer.

*Yes, he loves you.*

I take the game off my fingers, open it all up, lie it flat on your desk, read all of the answers at once.

*Yes, he loves you.*

*Yes, he loves you.*

*Yes, he loves you.*

*Yes, he loves you.*

All the way around.

**Kingwell**

LAST NIGHT I HAD MY FIFTH Mark Kingwell dream. I had my first one about a year ago, the next one about six months later, and the others in rapid succession. Last night, he was interrogating me, not in the capacity of a professor-student role, but more like we'd had a discussion as friends, and I had played the devil's advocate a little too inadequately for his taste. Which is weird, because Kingwell's not my friend. I don't even know him. I don't remember all of the dream, just that I was suddenly aware, as though outside of myself looking in, that I was dreaming about him and then suddenly I was inside myself again, looking at him while he was deep into his diatribe of the hermeneutic circle of authenticity or something.

I do remember this, though — the whole thing ended with him suddenly kissing me.

Yeah, I kissed him back.

So I'm in love with him. Does that matter? You don't know who I am. It would be easy for you to say, You're not in love with him, you're in love with his brain, his image, his media punditry, but you don't know that I was his neighbour once — for about a year and a half — and that I happened to be reading his treatise on happiness while I was falling out of love with one person and in love with another (no, not him), so that changes everything, doesn't it? Good.

To clarify, I am no longer his neighbour, and am no longer in love with the person I was falling in love with when I was reading that treatise on happiness. To clarify even further, I am no longer living in the same city as Mark Kingwell — in fact, I now live in a place that has no hope of ever harbouring someone like him, though it has other, more aesthetically pleasing qualities. I live in the foothills of the Rockies, just outside of Calgary. From my cabin, I stare at snow-covered peaks all day, listen to the Elbow

River run below a quiet highway and worry about things like cougar tracks and how much wood I'll have to chop before the storm they're calling for hits. And books. Where to get books out here? I read fiction and philosophy, mostly. Here, in this place, I am a less intense (if she's intense at all) version of Annie Dillard. I like her, too, though I've never had a dream about her in which she kisses me.

    I like it out here, but I miss Toronto sometimes — not so much the city itself (out here I have to apologize for being from there, and really have to work at punching through a presumption of elitism or frivolous unconscious demand that Torontonians seem to emit) — but its specific intellectual nature, which seems to be prized only by excessively self-conscious Torontonians. I'm a book designer — freelance, which means that even in Toronto I was able to work at home, and that my moving out here did not so much disrupt the amount of work I had as it did my visibility in the publishing scene. And Toronto is a city where visibility is paramount. Which is mostly why I left. To try my hand at hiding for a while, to see how it fit. In any case, I miss it sometimes, and that's probably why I had that dream about Kingwell last night. I've been out here for about six months now, and lately, I've been feeling a bit out of the loop, as Torontonians are prone to do when away from Toronto for any length of time. I spent the winter in my cabin, in all this silence, reading and absorbing other people's great ideas, notions, transcendences above the norm (in books brought from Toronto), and there's no one to talk about them with. Except Bob, the older guy who owns the hardware store in town, ten clicks down the river. He once ran away with a young, nubile, European thing and understands thinking of the non-cookie-cutter kind. But even he thinks I'm a little crazy. He asked me once, while we were having coffee in the back of his store, what I thought about going out for dinner, and I went off on some tirade about it being a way to merely apply a template of romance to one's life — about how "dinner and a movie" was really what a friend of mine calls "indiscriminate rigmarole" and how could those things possibly express a level of interest in someone that was superior to any other person you'd engaged in those very same activities with? And what did any of it signify? He finished his coffee in silence. It was only on my way back home that

I realized that he'd asked me out on a date. And that I needed to get out and talk to people more.

Out here, they call Toronto "the dot." I'm not sure why. <u>D</u>istrict <u>o</u>f <u>T</u>oronto? Because it's the biggest (and simultaneously most revered and resented) dot on our map? Because that's all it means west of Stratford? A dot? In any case, it's interesting to view Toronto from a place that really doesn't give a shit about it. Because that's exactly how the dot feels about the rest of Canada. A self-perpetuating prophecy. Or at least lots of noise playing back on itself in a big, giant loop. Feedback.

But if you're not from the dot, and don't read any of the "national" (read: dot-centric) newspapers and magazines, you may not know who Kingwell is. He's young. He's über-hip. He's a philosopher. Seriously. An honest-to-God live one. And if you're not from the dot, you may not know that for people from Toronto, it's important to make distinctions about who you know. Not only because that is just its style — you hang on to the name of every person you've met, because you may need their collaboration (in a creative, business-like kind of way) one day, or at the very least their help to get you further in some way — but because it's a big city, and so the likelihood of having an encounter with celebrity seems like a long shot, until you realize how many celebrities live in Toronto. I mean, Prince just bought a house there, for Christ's sake. But, as stated, this seems only important to Torontonians. And if you are one of those Torontonians, you know that your chances of meeting an intellectual celebrity in a neighbourhood called The Annex are greater than meeting a janitor, or a housewife, or a baker or a plumber there. I lived in The Annex. So does Kingwell. We were sandwiched in between Jane Jacobs and Stuart McLean and Naomi Klein, right across the street from Judy Rebick, though those names only mean something if you live in Toronto, as much as Torontonians like to think that there's a greater, ironically national-type importance attached to them.

Well, OK, technically speaking, we (Kingwell and I) did not live in The Annex. We were a few houses west of Bathurst, the official demarcation of The Annex/Not-The-Annex, but really, what's a few houses? We were in a neighbourhood called Seaton Village which, to our credit, was less expensive and even cooler than The Annex for a number of reasons (but only to Seaton Villagers): partly because The Annex was a place where it was impossible to live without employing that Toronto trait of needing to mention that you lived there and partly because Seaton Village was a place where those people who really knew how to sniff out a good place to live in Toronto lived. I lived in a crazy, maze-like building that was once alternately the Seaton Village municipal building and an asylum for the insane, pre-999 Queen Street West. Which will mean nothing to you if you grew up here, in the foothills of Alberta, or anywhere outside a hundred-mile radius of the dot.

At that point, I didn't know much about Kingwell. I had heard his name in conjunction with U of T a couple of times, and, in that typically Toronto fashion, hung on to the connection even though it was useless to me outside of potentially connecting the dots in a party conversation on which I might be eavesdropping. And if you work in publishing in Toronto, you know how many parties there are, and how many of them consist entirely of conversations more laden with names than actual words. It's surreal, almost like that scene in "Being John Malkovich" when Malkovich is inside his own head, except that the names change. Now that I think about it, it's amazing that I never saw Kingwell at one of those.

Regardless, I certainly didn't know what part of the city he lived in. I had just picked up his book on happiness, but I can't remember what drew me to it. Perhaps the fact that I was, to a great degree, depressed and elated simultaneously for the first time in my life. It was like being at both ends of the pendulum at once, and I tend to buy books blindly when in either one of those states, let alone both at the same time. Or maybe I just liked the idea of a philosopher. A good-looking one, just a handful of years older — enough to be attractive in a flawed, wiser-than-thou sort of way. In other words, a tangible, graspable one. Even if he was married. Socrates may have been cute for all I know, but really, what good was that to anyone, on the other side of the world, 2400 years later? So. Seaton Village. Apartment #7 in the former asylum. A sunny, unseasonably cold afternoon in September. Falling out of love and in love at the same time. Lying in bed reading Kingwell's book. He makes a reference to living near a certain intersection. I put the book down, hear the traffic rumbling through that certain intersection. I close my eyes and feel my heart stop. I take a deep breath. I start going through all the houses on my block in my head, and stop at the fourth one. That kind of brown, bricky one. Looks like all the others, really, in this area — a typically Toronto Annex house — tall and old and with some character, but not as Annex-y as some because, after all, we are in Seaton Village, which has more cement and cheap iron railings and phrases shouted in Italian and Portuguese. And Holy Christ, suddenly I'm his neighbour. I put the book away and listen to the traffic from that intersection and determine to spend the rest of the afternoon dreaming about him, until I remember the prism-like cast of my predicament. The blue of an ending relationship, the red of one just beginning and the blinding refraction of the proximity of celebrity that I hadn't even been aware of ten minutes before.

I think it was the whole notion of being a philosopher that intrigued me. I mean, how many *philosophers* do you meet in your life? And how do you go about casting aside those images of Socratic circles and togas that pop up in your head? It's sort of like getting to know a nun. You really want to, but you don't know how to go about it. And so I became obsessed with merely catching a glimpse of him. When I walked past his house, I'd imagine the glare gone from his windows and hope to arrest a view of the corner of a bookshelf warping under the burden of Russell, Kierkegaard, Spinoza, Descartes, Rousseau and a million other philosophers I knew I'd never read before I died. My, an existential thought. Must be contagion.

Personal sightings were few. He walked past once when I was in the laundromat around the corner, and I went out and watched him continue down the street, just to make sure. A couple of times I saw him sitting on his front step, reading thin, dense books and watching his cat pick its way through the flower bed. And while those incidences were certainly educational in terms of learning just how quickly my heart could pick up pace, they were not as telling as what I saw when I didn't see him. Which was, namely, an empty house.

Rarely a light on. Never him with anyone, which, for a philosopher, might not be as unusual as for someone with a more traditional job in Toronto, but nevertheless, when I walked by his house and looked at it, it felt as though it needed someone else in there with him. And the funny thing was, the more I read his book, which was an occasionally personal book, and the more one love replaced itself with another love, the more I thought to myself that there seemed to be a blindness to it, or, no, again a refraction — of a certain light coming in and him deflecting it to the other subjects despite the personal aspect to his treatise. Let me cut to the chase. About a third of the way through the book, and I don't know why (though reasons became apparent later on), I remember thinking, "My God, his marriage is falling apart."

Now, about that same time, it should have been obvious to me that my very own relationship with my newly instated lover was also doomed to disaster, but we stretched it out over eight more months and even an ocean. Just to make sure.

Which is neither here nor there, really — just proves my point about the ease of distraction at moments when one can least afford to be distracted, that's all. And reveals a certain empathy for our hero. The key to our respective happinesses, or at least contentednesses, lying in the very places we were ignoring.

Anyhow, a few months later, a few months after the breakup that should have happened before the relationship even started, I was at a dinner party at a friend's place (not in The Annex), and after all of the wine had been tucked away and everyone had left, I was helping her clean up and she was telling me about her new roommate, who wasn't there that night. (She worked at U of T, she said, but was doing research somewhere in Central America for the next few months.) It's great, she said, she's never around. She's either at the university 24/7, or in some other corner of the world. When did she leave? I asked. Oh, last week, she said, which reminds me — I have to drop off that envelope for her. I was drying the glasses. Actually, she said, it's on your way home. Can you do it? Sure, I said. And we finished the dishes and I put on my jacket and she gave me the envelope and I tucked it inside and we arranged to meet for coffee later in the week and then we said goodbye.

It was late, but I decided to walk home anyway, so I pulled the envelope out and looked at it, to see how close this place was that I needed to drop it off at. There wasn't quite enough light, so I walked down the street a bit and pulled the envelope out again under a street lamp. It said Mark K. The brown brick house's address underneath. I looked up, thought for a minute, looked down at the envelope again. Just to make sure. I looked up and down the street to see if anyone else was around. And then I threw my hands up in the air and danced down the block. I ran the rest of the way home.

And so there I was, at two in the morning, standing outside Kingwell's house. With a purpose. There was a light on in the back somewhere — I could see fingers of it slipping through to the front rooms. Now, clearly, I wasn't going to go up and ring the bell, but I mention this merely because there was a big mail slot in his door, so the sensible, two-in-the-morning thing for me to have done would have been to slip the envelope through the slot and have that be that. Right. Are you kidding me?

I hung on to that thing for nearly a week. Because I wanted to make sure that he was home when I delivered it. I wanted to be able to say something to him. I didn't have a clue what. But the next Saturday morning I woke up in a cheeky mood, and I figured, this is it. Do it now. So I had a shower, got dressed, decided not to have a coffee because I was jangly enough already. I walked out of Apartment 7, down the stairs and out of the former Seaton Village asylum. Cut across my lawn to Kingwell's house. Walked up the steps. Rang the bell.

I heard something in the back. I looked away for a moment, out onto the street. Looked back when I heard the lock on the door flick back. There he was. I smiled at him through the glass. He looked back at me, opened the door, pushed out the screen, kind of tilting his head. "I have something here from a colleague of yours," I told him. "Jane." I held the envelope out and he looked at it blankly. Then he remembered and started nodding his head. "I..." I started.

"Thanks," he said, opening the envelope and leaning back into his house so that the screen shut. I stood there. He had his back to me, pulling out papers from the envelope. Then he walked in, and kicked the door shut with the back of his foot. I looked away, out onto the street again. After a minute, I walked down the steps. I stood on the sidewalk for a while, facing the street, not sure I remembered which direction to turn to get home. Eventually, I decided on left and walked back to the former asylum. When I turned up the pathway, I looked back down the street toward Kingwell's place. And there he was. Standing on the sidewalk with the papers in his hand, staring after me.

That night was the first night I dreamt about him.

Oh. I get it now.
Toronto.
T.O.
T-dot.
The dot.

My friend Bob, the one who owns the hardware store ten clicks down the river, says that thinking about things like love never got anyone any further with it; that you still have to go through the same basic moves — falling in love, getting disillusioned, then falling out of love or being mistreated — whether you're philosophical about it or not, and that thinking about it doesn't stop you from making the same mistakes again. Funny thing is, he's one of the most pensive people I know. When he said that, I told him that he'd like reading Kingwell. He looked up at me for a while and then asked who Kingwell was.

I have his picture on my computer, Mark's. It's a goofy one, a leaning, grinning, shiny bald head. It comes up whenever I boot my computer, which is a laptop, so it comes with me everywhere I go. It's a small picture, the size of half my thumb, and I have it there as a bit of a joke, mostly because I've read enough of what he's written to assume he'd be mortified to know that his image pops up on someone's screen every day. He writes about commodification of culture a lot, enough that it makes it funny for me to do this, or witty, at least. Though he might argue, in a devil's-advocate kind of way, that true wit cannot be so blatantly manufactured, or thought out in such a Machiavellian fashion.

And out here, I have a lot of time to think about all of that. Out here, in all this physical and intellectual silence, where it's impossible to care about something like The Annex except in moments of nostalgia, I think a lot about why he gets poked around in the press so much. The people who do the poking say he deserves it — he's a media pundit, he brings it on himself — but if you look at it from his point of view, or perhaps, if you'll excuse my amateur approach to philosophy, a little less presumptuously (from a Jungian/Freudian perspective, say), it's a way for the journalist's unconscious to relieve repressed feelings of intellectual inadequacy (read: threat). You could draw the conclusion that some journalists are insecure when another writer uses their medium to say valuable things, as opposed to using it to publish acerbic expositions on our fair philosopher king's once- (voluntarily) bald head and goatee. And, clearly, they haven't dreamt of Kingwell like I've dreamt of him. Kingwell didn't finish his imaginary rant to them with a kiss. And they didn't kiss him back. Or maybe he did and they did and that's what's bothering them. Maybe even a pen as penis (envy) kind of scenario. In any case, what it comes down to is this: he makes us think about things that are worth thinking about. And that's threatening.

Because, I mean really, if you look at it, here's a guy who writes a book on something we all think we know something about — happiness — and right off the bat he says forget about that because you really don't. None of us does. And by the end of the book, which you figured he wrote to explain it, make it all a little more concrete, he's deconstructed it to a point where you haven't got a clue what happiness is anymore. It's not a feeling, or an emotion — it's this ephemeral state that has always, forever, been impossible for us to identify, namely because we're obsessed with deconstructing it with a view to identifying it.

I have a friend who takes photographs. I want to say "not your average photographs," but really what makes them not so average is how really *average* they are. They're photographs of normal things — of a rock, a piece of wood, a window, a dead bird, maybe. The thing about her subjects is that they're utterly ordinary, and she takes photos of them in an utterly ordinary way. No filters, no special lenses — she doesn't even worry about composition. And you know what? She wins awards for these things *all the time*. It baffles her. It doesn't baffle her husband so much ("Look," he says, "obviously you take pictures of things that people can relate to... things that they thought were simple, but aren't"), but it baffles her kids. Her most famous photograph is of her neighbour's garage. It's a pale-yellow garage, new, something he built himself, from a kit. Nothing special. And she says she was out on her porch one day, just after it had rained, and there was Lyle's garage, kind of bubbly through the raindrops on her porch screen, the light all low and grainy. So she took a photo of it. With a disposable camera. And she's constantly winning awards for this photo. She calls her kids up and says "I got another prize for Lyle's garage," and they all shake their heads. It really is an incredible photo. You look at it and you think, I'm looking at a garage. I am looking at a garage. And then you notice that it feels a bit out of focus, the photo, a bit blurry. And suddenly the raindrops on the porch screen draw themselves up to you and you can't see the garage anymore. But still, it is a photo of a garage. And poor Lyle? He's dead. Never got to see it. Which is kind of Socratic, in a way. It's all Socratic, this whole damn thing.

So this dream I had last night. The fifth one. I don't remember how we got there, but Kingwell and I are standing in this vacant parking lot somewhere in Toronto. It could have been somewhere around University and Richmond. And he's ranting at me but I'm not really listening — I'm kind of more taking in everything around me... the fact that he's in front of me ranting, the fact that we're in a parking lot in Toronto, and because it's empty, that has to mean that it's really really early in the morning, but it's light out and neither one of us is dressed all that warmly which must mean that it's summer. So suddenly I start thinking *I'm dreaming about Mark Kingwell and it's the longest day of the year.* And for some reason I keep repeating to myself, as though avoiding some sort of self-delusion or instinct toward mistrust, "everything is *okay* everything is *okay* everything is *okay.*" And I look at him and he stops talking mid-sentence and he looks back at me with those steely grey-blue eyes of his and he leans down and kisses me. On the lips. And I kiss him back. Yeah. When he pulls back, he's opening his eyes. He looks at me for a moment longer, then says "What now, huh?" and then he looks down, takes a security card out of a pocket, turns away and walks towards the back of a building at the other edge of the parking lot. He flashes his card at a big steel door set flush with the building and walks in. I'm alone. I'm alone at quarter-to-six in the morning on the longest day of the year, the sky crisp and blue and the air cool and clean, like Alberta air. *What now?* not even having occurred to me.

# The Offing

WHEN THE LIGHTS COME UP, we're the only two left in the theatre: a man and a woman. It's a matinee: *The Captive*, one of those French films that's so slow it leaves you gasping for air halfway through, and when it's over we both sit there digesting while teenaged ushers stand in the doorways behind us, waiting, unsure of what to do. She's about eight rows ahead of me and finally she turns around, blinks, ignores their pleading eyes, says out loud that it's fascinating how fixated the French are with placing afflictions on the banal. I'm not quite sure what she means, but nod and smile and say something to the effect of afflictions becoming so common that they *are* the banal, though I'm not sure I believe it. But she considers it and slowly, gracefully waggles her head in a way that says "perhaps," and we both get up and walk out.

In the lobby I feel compelled to make a fake call from the pay phone, "finishing up" just as she's coming out of the washroom. She sees me looking at her, walks over and says, I just realized I have an affliction for banal French films, so I suppose you're right.

We have some espresso at the little Portuguese dive on the corner of Commercial Drive, and talk for a long time. She tells me she grew up on a farm outside Vancouver and I ask if her parents still live there. She shakes her head, says it was repossessed a few years ago after her mother died and her father couldn't keep up the payments. I ask what happened to him, where he is now, but she turns her face to the window and gets lost in a thought. When we leave the espresso place, we turn a corner and there's a man with a small table on the sidewalk selling local strawberries — that's it. Nothing else. We can smell them halfway down the block, so we buy a punnet and begin to eat from it. After half a dozen berries, she puts her hand over mine, says No — let's wait, then ducks into a fish store run by a couple of Basque brothers. She walks along boards covered with shaved ice and stops in front of some sardines, shows me the blue gills that say they're very fresh and one of the brothers nods, says they've just come in, and grabs two handfuls for us and goes off to weigh them before we can say *yes, give us some*. We take them back to her place and put the sardines on a bed of salt, then put more salt on top and bake them. Crack the crust when they're done and it is heaven. All soft and tender. A little salt draws the moisture out of things, she says, but too much keeps it in, makes the liquid in a fish act against itself, conducting the heat to cook it. That's quite a metaphor, I say. She sprinkles the rest of the strawberries with smashed black peppercorns and she says *trust me* and I do.

★

It's not flirtation, you understand. Nothing so blunt as that. A friend of mine likes to describe himself and his girlfriend, who found each other in their early fifties, as having had all the sharp edges knocked off by the time they met. They'd just slipped into the company of one another, he said, without the anxiety and the games and the power struggles one has when younger and less trustful of the other person's motivation for attraction. That's how this thing with Sandra feels: interesting without a prelude to expectation, without the heart palpitations, obsession and imagination that can do your mind in, but still with a great deal of wonder. Something soft, the way a tick burrows under without you noticing, slowly infecting without the sharpness of a sting, or venom. Or the way persimmons ripen on a dormant tree, orange globes hanging from black, leafless branches like Christmas tree ornaments, losing their bitterness and becoming edible only after a heavy frost. To be honest, it's more a question of timing than desire. Right moment, nice woman, interesting place. Or right place, nice moment, interesting woman. Doesn't matter. And I'm glad. With expectation, there's always some salvage involved — salvage is essential to our universal tendency toward denial or fatally reshaping things to fit.

★

We sleep together. In the early morning, before dawn, a thunderstorm, an unusual one with a constant, hour-long rumble, wakes both of us up. The lights in her apartment flicker on, then off again. The one remaining candle by the bed snuffs out, a trail of upward-curling smoke visible in a crisp, metallic illumination of lightning. I squeeze Sandra. She sits up, looks at the candle burnt halfway down, says the ghost who occupies her apartment is in the room.

Can you feel her? she asks. There's a sharpness to the air when she's here.

I don't feel it. Not really.

Sandra looks out of the window for a while and when the thunder finally fades and the moon comes out again, she lies back down beside me, says It's OK, and falls asleep.

A few hours later, while we're having coffee at the table by the window in her kitchen, looking out onto the street, she tells me that the apartment building was a convent before the war — *the first one*, she specifies, though there have been so many in the past century I can't be entirely sure which war she means — and that there were tunnels connecting it to the church that used to be on the next block so that the nuns could pass between buildings without being seen in public.

They're blocked off now, she says, but when I first moved in here the ghost was unhappy and the man who has the apartment in the basement next to the tunnel would hear her running back and forth in it at night, feet slapping in the hollow of the passageway. But she only shows up here now, and in much calmer ways.

I look out at the street. The building where the church used to be is boarded up and some skater kids are practising their tricks on its short railings. A large branch of a tree fell on its roof in the storm last night; the branch dangles over the front stair with a gash of white wood exposed, and there's a shock in seeing this. I've always thought that wounds like this are best reserved for the obscured vision of night time. Or fog, where you can retreat from the surprise, the shock, or even question what you're seeing.

Sandra laughs. I look over at her, away from the window, and she smiles at my concentration, puts her hand on my cheek and leaves it there.

*

I'm a biologist, but don't talk much to Sandra about my work. Science with so much terminology based in Latin derivatives doesn't make for scintillating conversation with many people. She's an etymologist, knows the origins of things and enough Latin to hold her own, but she's the quiet, bookish type you might imagine, and doesn't talk about what she does very often either. Once in a while it comes up in conversation, though. Like the other night when we were discussing the movement of stars and she said that both the words *zenith* and *azimuth* come from Arabic, the first meaning "the way" or "direction" and the other meaning "path over the head."

I didn't know that.

She's not like the women I've gone out with before. She's quiet, possibly shy, but she knows the things she would and wouldn't do. She's known from a very early age, I suspect. Her passion in bed is unexpected and authentic; in her refusal to engage in social conformity of the safely nonconformist kind, she defies prediction and categorization. Funny.

*

Take a big mirror and lay it flat. Then lie down and blow on it and watch how the condensation of your breath fans out, then fades away. That's what the ocean is today; flat and shimmery as glass. A general haze gives the impression of being in the middle of a blank canvas, or a painting that Turner has just begun — one brushstroke to establish the horizon and that's it. The horizon very distant at that.

Water as flat as this sometimes makes for the best fishing, but I haven't brought my gear. I lived for a time on the Rideau Canal, sharing a cabin with a friend during the first few summers after university, and when the water was like this, we would go fishing. Each time we left the cabin with our rods and worms and bacon cut into strips small enough to drape over a hook once and back again, Marc would issue his disclaimer: "You bait your own hook, and you kill the fish you catch." The funny thing is, I have never caught a fish. Not in my whole life. Marc seemed to think it was because I lacked conviction, and when I tell Sandra that, she says she can never start an outboard — or open tightly sealed jars — because she isn't confident that she can. I reckon they're both right. I'm not sure what I'd do with a live fish in my hands, knowing that I'd have to finish the job. I suspect I wouldn't be able to club its head against the side of the boat, nor to force the hook out of its body so that it might swim free. And if I'm wrong about that, do I really want to know? Marc always said, "You'd be surprised. People who've never killed anything are the worst. Once they get the courage up to club the thing, they can't stop, won't stop, until the fish is pulp. They ruin the fish. The thing with killing," he'd say, "is you want to keep it clean."

There are cormorants skimming the surface of the water in long, thin lines. One after the other. I can see that she's mesmerized by them, has lost track of what time it is. The surface of the sand is scattered with strands of mussels clinging to seaweed and tiny seashells whose colours remind me of the rings of Saturn. My hand is filled with black spears that look like a written Arabic "2."

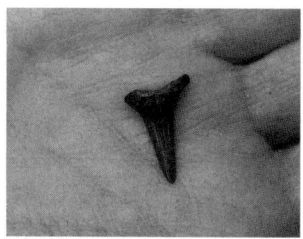

Like that.

We're looking for fossilized shark teeth. The entrance to the bay is dredged every once in a while and when it is, shark teeth — six million years old from the bottom of the ocean — show up on shore. There's a certain glint you have to look for, I say to Sandra. We walk with our heads down and after an hour or so, she starts to recognize that glint of light the teeth give and we find some nearly ten centimetres long. She walks over the tiny saturned seashells. I used to have a friend who had been through so many relationships that ended badly, he no longer found solace in looking at beautiful women. *They have no effect anymore,* he said, and when I look at these shells I understand what he meant. You realize that you're more attracted to imperfection: the shell which is pretty, but detached or broken; the rock which looks richer wet than dry. Take the nautilus shell, for example. It is, in a lot of ways, perfection. Tightly coiled, expanding outward in exact gradients, it's frequently regarded as something to aspire to as a model of proportion. But in the ammonite, a sort of fossilized nautilus, the membranes that separate the chambers are asymmetrically wavy, instead of straight, and the colour gradations, while beautiful, are hardly consistent, as though time has compressed the perfection of the shell into something more interesting. The outside is still a perfect spiral, but the inside — the individual chambers, what the perfection is composed of — is a series of compacted formerly-perfects. Dissect the fossil and you see the weight of history that altered it. I prefer the honesty of the ammonite to the perfection of the live nautilus, prefer the lack of motivation toward the unflawed that the ammonite contains.

Sandra looks at me in a way that says she's not quite sure what to make of me, or these shark teeth, these things that have a fluid beauty which belies the sharpness of their edges, and purpose. The sand is scattered with necklaces of pebbles and algae, the first caught in the last, and she picks up a strand and wraps one around her wrist. Beaches are filled with them, these perfect imperfections. That's why I come here. That's why I brought her here with me.

We walk along the shore to a place where a local guy named Skinny Jimmy used to live. He's a musician who drives a pink Cadillac with a cross mounted on the grille. After a while we get to a thin, elusive bay, camouflaged by grey granite sticking up in shards across its opening. It feels like Moby Dick, with all the large-scale mammalian parts in metaphor: nostrils and mouths and the teeth we're wending our way through.

The water gets shallower and shallower and soon we have to walk to skirt the high, steep rocks on shore. Around a corner a house appears, or rather a grand shack made of weather-beaten boards and additions, more like a sculptural experiment in driftwood than a dwelling. A small boat with a cabin, the kind you used to see on *The Beachcombers*, is stranded and tilted on the stony shore well above the high-tide line.

The shack has long since been abandoned, its windows smashed by bored local teenagers. I tell Sandra that Skinny Jimmy gave this place up for the pink Caddy, that he moved out once all the kids were grown and lives in that white house just across from the liquor agent near the harbour now. I try to imagine raising four or five children, all alone, at the end of this narrow bay protected by shards of rock. A tire on a rope still hangs out on a beam by the house.

We look through the couple of feet of clear, cold water we're in and wonder whether we should gather some oysters. She tells me a funny story she read the other day in a magazine where the writer had been in the north of France with a friend who was a gourmand. They were slurping back enormous, seventy-year-old oysters and after much thought the only negative thing the friend had to say about them was, "These would be difficult to eat in a car." I laugh and we're distracted and forget about them.

We head back to the beach and the haze is turning to dusk. There are small patches of breeze on the surface of the water, appearing, disappearing, like memory.

Sandra walks ahead of me, holding her arm up, victorious, when she finds one last shark tooth in the waning light. She turns and smiles. The heat from the sun and her skin has cracked the bracelet of seaweed and it falls off. The cormorants skim the surface of the water in long, thin lines.

★

A few nights later, we have dinner at her house. It's a long and languorous one, with crusty Persian rice and more than one bottle of wine. I'm sitting back having a sip of the wine when one of the postcards she has covering an entire wall of her living room falls down. Sandra ignores it. Another postcard falls. She looks up at me, then turns and looks at the wall behind her. What's up, I say, and she turns back and tilts her head in an apologetic half-smile.

I get up to wash my hands. When I turn the bathroom light on, it flickers and dies. Sandra sighs and finds some matches and lights some candles.

Doesn't it bother you? I ask later, when we're in bed. Her head is between my shoulder and chest and she shakes it back and forth once.

She's a good ghost, she says, just a little troubled. The radiator clangs beside us. I think she may have been a postulant, she says. She seems to not like men here, and in my experience those who are young and learning are less forgiving than those who have lived through teaching the young and unforgiving.

I like the idea of that, I say, smiling.

Yeah, she says, turning her face to the window and reaching her arm up, fingering the air.

The radiator clanks again, and a train passes on the tracks a few blocks away, and then everything is quiet, the kind of quiet where you think you can hear it all happening, all the things that have no sound. Minds working, persimmons turning sweet, fish breathing underwater, sleep.

★

When I leave for work in the morning, she's still sleeping. I call in the evening, just before leaving the lab, but there's no answer. I drive by, see a light in her window and idle across the street until I see her figure move across it. I don't buzz or go up.

I try calling over the next couple of days but her phone is out of service. I go by a few times, but see no shadows or silhouettes in her window. I ring the bell to her place: no answer.

Bertolucci's *I Sognatori* is playing at the cinema and I go to a matinee on the weekend, but I'm bored by all the perfection on the screen — the flawless faces, bodies and filming — and spend the time craning my neck around and straining my eyes to see if Sandra's in the theatre. We've never talked about Bertolucci but there's a lot of his imagery in her sparse language — the rawness of desire coupled with the smoothed edges of beauty — and I can imagine her liking him.

The theatre holds about twenty people, none of them her.

The next day, I buy fresh figs from Turkey at the market and try eating them with smashed black pepper, like we did with the strawberries, and they're delicious, supple and sharp at the same time. I have to remember to tell her that.

★

I sleep with someone else while I'm away at a convention. The whole thing is such a cliché — *the boring seminars, harmless flirtation, too much alcohol, harder to stop it than to just get it over with* — that it slips from my memory nearly as soon as the woman — someone I know I'll never see again — leaves my room. *Click* goes the door jamb and I turn on the television to watch the five a.m. news. The woman flashes back into my memory at the airport when I instinctively look for Sandra's face in the crowd. She's not there, of course, and I watch the luggage carousel go round and round. Chuck-chink. Chuck-chink. Chuck-chink.

★

There's a message from Sandra when I get home. I call her. A soft, cool breeze, almost undetectable, comes through the room and I turn to see if I'd forgotten to shut a window while I was away. Her phone rings. She picks up.

Your number was out of service, I tell her.

Yes, that happens sometimes. It tends to fix itself, though, she says.

The ghost? I ask.

Maybe, she says. There's a long pause. My father died, she says. I had to take care of things.

Oh... I'm sorry... You should have called earlier. I could have helped.

There wasn't much to do, really.

Are you OK?

I'm fine. But I'd like to have a nice dinner tonight and think about something else. Can you come over? Can we do that?

Of course. I'll be there around seven.

Make it six. And bring some *harissa*.

I arrive just after six and she's already halfway through roasting a chicken. I have some of my gin-marinated olives that she likes. Her face lights up when she sees them and she tries opening the jar but the seal is strong. She runs hot water over it, bangs on the lid with a hammer, then gives up and finally hands it to me. I open it with a loud pop and she looks annoyed, but takes an olive, grins, and sets me to making a carrot salad with some *ras-al-hanout*.

It's a fine meal, with the fading light casting a dusty pallor across the room. It's the week in August when, after two months of ignoring the inevitable, you begin to notice the days getting shorter. In a darkening corner by the door, I notice an urn. She sees me looking at it.

He wanted his ashes to be scattered at the farm.

You don't talk much about him.

Things kind of fell apart...

Oh.

She's silent for a while, then looks out the window, her hands in her lap.

It's completely dark outside now. The streetlights have sprung on and the staircase of the building across the street is lit in a pale yellow sheen, the kind of light that shows the flaws in things. The lopsided railing by the stairs, the crumbling at the outside edge of them. I wonder if skateboards can do that kind of damage or if it's just age and neglect.

Sandra is staring out the window too, down the street to the lights of the skyscrapers. Are you doing anything tomorrow? I ask.

She shakes her head.

Then let's take him to the farm.

She looks at me, blinks slowly and presses her lips together. And nods.

## The Offing

★

We drive out past Sumas, the town closest to the farm. The land is flat at first, then rolling hills. The fields around are successive shades of green — fronds of barley moving evenly in the wind like waves, the occasional rogue plant stuck up in the middle of it all, not moving.

It's a landscape I can't shake; it intrigues me more than the traditional dramatic ones — mountains, seaside cliffs, deserts. Rolling hills appear in my dreams as the only landscape I remember and I can't say why. It must be a sort of nostalgia, Sandra says.

The first summer hay is ready, and we pass a field being harvested by a guy in a big combine. At the corner of the field, about two yards into the cut hay, there's an old man sitting on one of those electric carts with handlebars and a basket in the back, the kind you get when you can't walk so well anymore. He's parked and looking out at the field with his hands on the handlebars while the blades on the combine whir and create a kaleidoscope of chaff and dust and grain. The old man is wearing a baseball cap and his head is turned away from us, facing the field. I wonder if he's an old farmer forced into retirement by some sort of repetitive motion injury, who drives himself along the highway in his cart to a field when the nostalgia becomes unbearable. Or maybe he's just bored and out for a drive, interested in the mechanics of the combine the way old engineers stand for hours at the windows cut out of the solid fences where foundations for a skyscraper are being poured. Or maybe the guy in the combine is his son and he's just watching him, can't let go.

Sandra's looking at a road map and asking questions and at the speed we're travelling the old man and even the field are quickly out of the sight of the rearview mirror. She wants to go for a walk at a ridge nearby before going to the farm, so we drive on for twenty more minutes, then park at a trailhead she knows and start walking, leaving the urn on the back seat.

We walk through the forest and cross some fields, gingerly stepping over fences on the small ladders built for hikers like us. The forest is mostly birch and I tell Sandra they're one of my favourite trees. She asks why and I tell her it's because there've been times when I've fallen asleep in a copse of them and woken thinking I was inside an enormous diamond, so hopeful is the light they let in. She laughs and says she was expecting some sort of scientific or biological reason, like how the cells in its cross-section line up or something.

I laugh and say that if the temperature and humidity are right, and the forest is quiet enough, you can hear birchbark cracking.

Cracking? she asks.

Away from the trunk, I say. Peeling itself back. Revealing a younger layer.

She tells me about a time, one December back east, when she heard the *tock* — she makes a sharp sound with her tongue against the roof of her mouth — of the sap in a maple freezing and how it echoed through the stillness, one tree at a time all around her in stereophonic sound, and how she could not imagine a sound more pure.

I smile.

We come into a denser part of the forest and walk through it in silence. She takes my hand and we wind around the topography of larger humps in the landscape. I'm starting to feel a bit claustrophobic from the tightness of the trail when Sandra stops and drops my hand. I think she senses my claustrophobia, but when I turn to look at her she's very pale and is staring off to the left. She begins walking determinedly. I follow. I see a flash of white at the forest's edge and she stops, breathing hard. I walk off the trail a bit to get a better view. I come around a clump of trees. There's a white dress hanging from the low branch of a Jack pine. I look back at Sandra and she says Do you see that too? And I nod.

Please go and touch it, she says, so I know it's real.

I walk slowly over the forest floor, snapping branches and crushing pine needles. A heady scent rises from them which stops when I do, at the dress. A wedding dress. I reach out and finger the fabric — a dull, rough silk — and take the edge of it between my forefinger and thumb, pull it so the skirt stretches out into the air and she can see that it's real. She nods and looks away.

By the time I get back to her the colour has returned to her face. She pulls me in another direction, away from the dress, the brand-new dress, the dress which looks as though it has never been worn, save for a tiny scuff of dirt and blood at the armpit. The kind you'd get from a cut made shaving.

We walk to the edge of the forest, to some boulders. The ground dips a little and a few hundred feet off we can see the rim of the ridge. We head towards it.

Near the edge, Sandra stops walking. She stands, looking at the view, and puts her hand up to shade her eyes from the sun and her hair, which is tracing itself around her face in the breeze. I continue, walk right to the edge and look over, feeling the tingle of vertigo in my feet. I peer past rocky ledges to a sparkly trickle of a stream set in a clump of cottonwood six or seven hundred feet below.

I look up, out over the land farther away. The edge of a large lake is visible, and the farmland leading to it is neatly laid out in squares, some yellow, some green, some brown.

Why do you think it was there? Sandra calls from behind me.

I don't know, I say. I look at her and she's no longer shading her eyes, but standing there in the full sun, wind whipping her hair across her face in elliptical patterns. *I don't know.*

Come have a look, I say, looking at the river. I hear her rustling slowly through the grass and when she gets to the edge she nods slowly. Did you know, she says, that if you raise yourself six feet in the sky you can see two more miles of land, you can add two miles to your horizon? Then she turns around, takes one step back away from the edge and collapses.

I catch her by the shoulders just before she hits the ground. Her head lolls over the edge and I quickly pull her back by the ankles, her jeans rising up her calves. Her hair is across her face and I clear it, pinch her cheeks, shake her wrists, calling SandraSandra as I do. SandraSandra.

After a minute, her eyes move beneath her eyelids and she opens them, squints, turning her head away from me. She asks for chocolate, says there's some in her bag. I choose one of the seven or eight partially eaten bars in there and feed her pieces of it until it's gone and she lies there, sucking on the last piece, looking away — and I hold her and don't once stop looking at her, don't once look up and out at the land and the lake far in the background, the one we're so high above, don't even feel tempted by it as I once might have.

She sits up, rests her head on her knees, says thank you. She smiles and squeezes my hand. Closes her eyes and says I guess I'm afraid of heights. It comes and goes. Sometimes it's OK. Sometimes it's bad. It's bad when there's stress.

Oh, I say. We're silent and then the wind gusts and all you can hear is the tall grass brushing up against itself.

We walk slowly back to the car, avoiding the forest, zigzagging over the grid of farmer's fields on top of the ridge, passing through rye, sugar beets, canola. She walks straight into a cornfield. I follow, thinking I'm going to see her take a cob from the stalk, peel back the husk and silk and eat it raw then and there, the way I heard Katharine Hepburn used to. But she just wants to look at it, to touch it, to feel it on her hands.

We're standing, looking at each other, our bodies hidden by the corn, two human heads bobbing on top of stalks. I laugh, and hold her, and I wonder if it's nostalgia that made her walk into the field, touch the corn.

When we turn to head back to the car I see a scarecrow at the edge of the field but then it waves and I realize it's a farmer. She raises her hand, then drops it and takes mine while we walk to the road. A truck transporting pigs swooshes past when we get to the shoulder. We stand in the dust and even in the hundred-kilometre-per-hour eddy of wind you can hear the pigs stomping and squealing and she drops my hand to shade her eyes.

★

## The Offing

We drive and when we get to the farm, I park on the shoulder of the highway, by the driveway. She's happy to see that the farm is still a farm and as we sit parked on the shoulder of the road beside it, she rolls down her window, places her forearms across the ledge and rests her chin there, looking at the house to the right where a string of fresh laundry puffs and swings in the breeze. There's no noise — no voices, no dogs barking, no machinery running, no radio blaring from inside the barn. After a while she pushes herself away from the window, gets out of the car and begins walking down the long driveway toward the house. I open my door and get out and when I shut it to follow her, she stops walking, turns around and looks at me. I reach in through the open back window and take the urn. Follow her down the driveway.

There's no one at the house, but she doesn't want to have to come back, thinks if we just scatter the ashes in the pear orchard behind the barn the owners will never notice, especially with this breeze to spread it around. They've let the orchard go anyway, she says, pointing to the trees, which look wiry, unruly.

We walk to one of the middle rows and I hand her the urn. She struggles with the lid. Are you OK? I ask. Yeah, I just can't get it open, she says.

I take it from her gently and twist. The lid is fast. I put the urn between my legs and wrench on the top with both of my hands. Nothing.

She starts breathing hard, staring at the urn. I try again. Nope, I say, and put it on the ground.

It happens all the time, I say. I had to saw my mother's open.

She looks at me and turns and walks back to the car, gazes at the house once more, gets in and says Let's go. I apologize, but she waves her hand, says she's not angry, she just wants to go home. I put the urn in the back, open my door and stare out over the highway. There's a giant hare charging across the neighbour's cut field, between the cows. I wave at a man standing at the edge of the cornfield but it's a scarecrow and Sandra turns and smiles in a tired kind of way when she sees my arm go up.

On the drive back, there's a wind farm on the horizon, and a nuclear cooling tower, and a hot-air balloon in the sky. We pass the hayfield, coming at it from a different angle, and the hay is all cut, the combine is gone and the old man isn't there anymore.

★

You don't feel the bite of a tick. It slowly, secretly, inserts its pincers into your skin and begins to feed without you noticing. If you do notice it, it'll be too late to merely brush it off — its pincers will stay lodged in your skin and infect it, possibly with the madness that comes with Lyme disease. If the tick goes undetected, it will feed for a couple of days, blowing up to ten times the size it was before it found you, then slowly, painlessly extract its pincers and fall off, happy and satisfied. The small bruise it leaves will look like a bull's eye. That's how you know if you've been bitten. Bull's eye.

Sandra seems exhausted, but insists I come up to her place for dinner. There's some veal and small onions in her fridge, some tomatoes and a bottle of red Languedoc in her pantry, so I make a stifado. The television is working, and we watch the news while the stew cooks. I sit on the couch and she sits on the floor between my legs. My hand is on her shoulder and when I run it absent-mindedly up her neck, my thumb grazes something hard. I pull her hair up and lean over, see the tick on the back of her neck.

It's dug in already. I squeeze it by the head to try to get it to let go, then pull gently. What are you doing? she asks.

Hold still, I say, and the tick comes out, pincers and all. I show it to her and she stretches her lips. *Yeesh.* Her hand goes up to her neck and she feels the bump, asks if it will go away.

Yes, I say. You'll be all right. She turns back to the news and I get up, throw the tick in the sink in the bathroom, whose lights flicker, and go to the kitchen to stir the stifado.

★

At four in the morning she sits straight up, accidentally jamming her knee in my thigh as she does, and I bolt up too. A beam of opaque moonlight is coming across the bed, across her face, and when I look at her, I see sweat on the sides of her nose, a sharp glistening in pale air. I ask if she's OK, put my hand between her shoulder blades. She nods, staring straight ahead.

The ghost? I ask.

She shakes her head. Bad dream, she says. She sighs.

# The Offing

There was a long, grassy hill, she says. Sunshine. Everything lush and green. The sky damp, but blue and puffy white, like after a good rain. I was wearing the dress and it was loose and it swung around me as though my arms in its sleeves didn't matter.

My father, me, one other person... a lanky, athletic blonde — a landscaper. She was cutting the grass. That seemed odd. It was a big, rolling hill. Perhaps a field, once, with a large oak tree at the top of it, like the one at the beginning of the title sequence of *Six Feet Under*, you know? All you could see was hill.

My father was telling the blonde what to do. Don't cut too closely around the edges, he said. There were no edges, but when he said that, it was clear to me that that was where I was going to die in a moment, within the hour, anyway, that there was a hole behind me and I'd lie down in it and someone would begin to throw dirt on top of me and the view would go from blue to white to speckled with black to nothing at all. Just weight. And then nothing.

I turned to see the hole and there was nothing there. Nothing dug, but no grass either. Just a blank spot. As though it was invisible, or unavailable. My father was rushing around, getting things ready. It wasn't clear what. There was no panic, though, no macabre feeling. It felt quite calm and matter-of-fact, as though everything had been decided. When it would end, where, how, with (or without) whom. It seemed quite civil. The blonde moved farther and farther away with her Whippersnipper and my father kept making circles of a tighter and tighter circumference — nothing in his hands, but he was busy. And I just stood there thinking, *this is it, and that's OK.* I wondered for a long time how it would feel to have the dirt thrown on me. What kind of a weight it would have — and how long I would have to think about that while lying down in the hole. How long it would take before the dirt would cover my face.

My father was not very pleased, but he was quiet. The only words he said were to the woman. *Don't cut too closely around the edges.* At one point when he was in the middle of his circles I looked at him and he looked up at me but then he looked away. And all I could think of was the weight of dirt.

And then I rose up, above everything, above my father, above the hill, and everything looked so small, the farms all fingering out and away, toward the sea, and I said to him that the part of the sea closest to the horizon, the more distant part of the sea in sight, is called the offing... and when I reached the top I could see farther than I ever thought a horizon could allow, and it was all water... every single inch.

Her legs are shaking and I hold her and tell her she's home, she's safe. All the lights in her apartment come on and she nods and says I know, I know and when she falls asleep again half an hour later they're still on.

I think of the graves of some Roma I saw once, where the deceased were depicted on their tombstones in some final action, a ritual of permanence, a finalization of character — standing in front of the car they loved, playing cards, tending a donkey.

I thought, seeing them, that it's probably better we don't get to see how we're represented after we die. The surprise, or the disappointment, would probably be too much to bear. The nautilus versus the ammonite; the straight, empty chamber versus the imperfect, compressed one. Who you think you are versus who you are.

I only notice the lights are out when the room is filled with enough daylight to see the shadow of the radiator start to form on the floor. The radiator clanks. A train passes on the tracks a few blocks away.

## The Offing

★

The fig is a plant whose blossom is hidden inside its fruit. Its tree doesn't flower, but the fruit wouldn't exist if it did. Tiny wasps crawl in and out of the hole at its apex, leaving it sticky and sweet, all strawberry and honey inside the thin skin. I love that skin, so thin and easily bruised. You think if you touch it, juice will appear on your fingers, but when you scrape the skin back, you find a surprisingly thick layer of pith that holds the fruit and seeds in.

I drive out past the farm and take a walk through the birch forest again. A fox watches me warily from outside its hole. I notice her first, panting, looking around. Then she scans over to me, stops her tongue moving, brings her lower mouth up, closed, and stares, her ears twitching, alert. I back off, take another way around, laughing when I remember that foxes double back too, to watch the hunters closing in on them. I can't find the wedding dress in the trees, though I do see a lot of tracks beneath a Jack pine which could have been the one it was hanging from. I think about the ghost and how it's there, against your will, and the only way to deal with it is to live with it or remove yourself from it, to take yourself away. How ghosts don't follow — they inhabit.

From the top of the ridge, near where Sandra fainted, I see the edge of that lake below again, diamonding light up from its surface, and wonder if that classifies as an offing. I walk back to the car and drive down through the farms to it, park at its edge. I sit thinking, and after a while I notice a tangle of fishing line on the shore, light blue against the small strip of sand. I get out of the car and fashion a fishing rod out of a branch and the line. It doesn't take long to untangle, and there's still a hook attached — an old-fashioned, rusty one, but a hook nonetheless. I pull the line tight.

I sit on the shore in the failing light, casting the way Marc taught me. The surface of the water is sparsely pocked with the round ripples of fish feeding... it's the right time of day.

I feel a tug, and jerk my arms high and fast to set the hook, but because I don't have a reel, I'm not sure what to do next. I haul the branch low to the ground, keeping the tension steady, then stand on it while bringing the line in with both of my hands. The fish fights a bit, but not as much as I've seen them fight on Marc's lines, not as much as I would have expected.

I pull the fish out of the water and it wriggles away from the hand I have out to steady it on the line. The hook is caught in its lower lip and as I hold the line up, it stops flapping and looks at me with its right eye, gills expanding and contracting, expanding and contracting.

I sit down and try to get the hook out, but it's barbed. I put the fish on the sand, where it immediately starts flapping again, and go to the car, to the glove compartment, where I have a pair of pliers.

The fish is flapping slower and slower and when I get back to it, it stops, looking at me again, breathing, as I grab its head and cut through the hook. I think of watching a fisherman in Norway once, as he simply threw the fish he was catching over his shoulder to let them die slowly, on the land. In essence, suffocating them. At the time suffocation versus being clubbed to death seemed reasonable, like Sandra wondering only what the dirt on her face would feel like when she saw her own grave, instead of thinking about the violence of dying. *The thing with killing is, you want to keep it clean.* But I'm not so sure now.

The fish has another flapping fit, which looks like it might be its last. I watch the fish flap closer and closer to the water's edge, and I'm still not sure what I'm going to do. But when it gets nearly there in one last jump and lies with its mouth half in the water, breathing, breathing, I get up. I pick up the fish and walk into the water. I let it go, let it slip from my hands in the water made opaque by a darkening sky, where it's hard to tell where lake and air meet. Where it's hard to see the horizon, let alone the offing.

It's completely dark when I pass the farm on the way back. I pull over on the shoulder beside it, windows rolled down. There's a single light on in the house, on the top floor in the window beneath the roof's peak, but no noise. Crickets creaking and fireflies flashing against the windshield, but no human noise.

I get out of the car, take the urn from the back seat and open the trunk. There's a shovel I keep in there for emergencies, though not usually ones like this. I take it out and walk to the orchard, trying to stay out of the light. I pick a nice pear tree at the back corner of the orchard and start to dig. The dirt is soft and easy and within a few minutes I have a hole deep enough to rest the urn in.

I think of my mother, who gave in to bone cancer, her strength dissolving so fast you could watch it. I still feel her every now and then, even though I'm not spiritually inclined. A breeze will slip past and I'll feel her say hello to me, and ask how I'm doing. Just fine, I always say.

I think about the dress, how a breeze caught it after I'd let it go and I felt something pass me, something not real, not there — or barely there, like a spider web cut from its anchor, floating down, a single thread of miniscule silk — tangible, but untouchable. The skirt stayed stiff as though starched, billowing like a sail when the wind hit it and turned it sideways. I thought I saw one of the arms flip up, as though to calm an unnecessary agitation, but then the dress went limp and hung by its neck from the branch again, lifeless, and the wind slipped past my elbow and was gone.

*Just fine.*

A brief pause at the skyline and the dead appear again in your life as a memory.

I fill the hole, walk back to the car and shut the trunk quietly. When I get back to the coast I pull over at the shore of a small beach near Skinny Jimmy's. I get out, leaning against the warm hood of the car with my hands in my pockets, looking up at the stars, the engine ticking as it cools.

I hear a couple of people, a man and a woman, farther down the shore, splashing and talking.

*... beside him...*

*... turned over...*

*yeah, but...*

*hahahahaha...*

*... a HUGE frog...*

*You did?...*

More splashing. Bursts of laughter between moments of silence, which I imagine involves long, languorous kissing. I hope it does. I walk to the edge of the water and feel a breeze ripple up, through my shirt. The moon has risen a couple hundred feet off to the side and in the moonlight I can see the sparkle of tiny waterdrops on the couple, laid across their skin like phosphorescence. All the beach is glistening with broken oyster shells, sanded smooth. I lean over and begin to gather oysters for Sandra, plucking them out of the water, still rough, edges sharp enough to cut you deep. I turn one over in my hand and I think *this*, this is where pearls come from. I don't care that they don't, or that freshwater pearls come from mussels, not oysters, and that the pearl is created as a response to a parasite, not just a simple grain of sand, like we're told. I care that if you raise yourself six feet in the sky you can see two more miles of land, you can add two miles to your horizon.

**postcard**

*postcard*

Toronto. The mid-'70s. A housewife and a luthier. Their two children, Anna and Sophia. Eight and six. Skating around City Hall, the newly erected CN Tower hovering behind them. A Super 8 camera on a tripod, filming them so neither one of them is missing from the frame at any time. They skate round and round soundtrackless, in washed-out colour. Round and round. Striped woollen hats and mitts with strings. Thick snowpants. Breath rising. They are four. Suddenly they are three. Anna tripping quickly toward the camera on her skates, grinning. Tripping past the frame. The camera shakes. Zooms in on Sophia, follows her closely around the rink. Stops when she passes her parents, who are two. Standing face to face. Fighting. Sophia's head passes through the frame every thirty seconds. Round and round.

*1993. France. In the centre of a village, sitting on the edge of a fountain, the place filled with tired, dusty men in leather vests, rifles slung over shoulders, taking swigs from a stone jug of wine. It's hunting season and I'm sitting next to one of the men and his catch of a few floppy*

An audio tape. *"Describe blue."* The luthier.
*"What?"* Me. A game we used to play. The word game.
*"Pretend you're speaking to someone who doesn't know what colour is, Sophia, someone who can't see... describe blue to her."*
*"Hmmm... blue is... a deep lake... and the sky."*
*"What's a lake?"*
*"What?"*
*"I can't see. 'Lake' is no good to me. Describe how blue feels."*
*"Blue is... cool... like wind hitting your cheek."* Me blowing on his cheek.
*"It's like... when you rub my feet."* The shhhh *of material rubbing.* *"It's coming home — after school, the way this house smells."*
*"Mmmm."*
A kiss. (A peck.)
*"Sweet dreams."*
*"What do they say in Iran again?"*
*"asoodeh bekhab..."*
*"What does that mean?"*
*"I wish your sleep to be peaceful and worry-free."*

rabbits, hanging down from his old leather bag, long ears grazing cobblestone. At an épicerie on the other side of the square, the woman who ran it had some cheese pastries she'd made and I

*postcard*

A Christmas party. Our neighbours. Ron and Vicki, who drive a brown Dart and have two small, yappy poodles in lieu of children. Ron's got his shirt unbuttoned halfway down his chest; some frothy brown hair is spilling out. I think there are medallions buried in there somewhere and I'm wide-eyed and terrified for the first time by someone's sexual predacity. Even though I'm only eight. Vicki is looking at her husband constantly, drink always held high and tilted toward her, speaking to our mother out of the corner of her mouth. They just moved in. Ron is talking to Mrs. Milne (who is leggy, thin, a piano teacher who drives a Datsun 380 ZX). He laughs like a TV anchor, all robust but empty and fake, resisting trauma. Vicki is moving her lips at our mother, but I can't hear what she's asking.

"Guitars and violins," our mother brays. We're on the other side of the room, but she says it loud enough that it makes us look over at her. She's laughing too, but not like Ron. Laughing like she's making fun of someone. Our father's standing by a card table that has an enormous bowl of Bits & Bites on it and he's just closed his eyes for a second too long; you can see a vein throbbing in his right temple. His eyelids twitch and he looks over at us, sees us looking over at her, then stutters a question to Mr. Milne, who's staring sorrowfully into the bowl of snacks. I can't hear what he asks him either, but Mr. Milne just looks up at our father and smiles smally.

"…used to be romantic, I thought…" Our mother. "A luthier, after all. Like a poet. Only with wood. That's what he used to say, anyway."

Our father — the whole room, as a matter of fact — is staring at her. The ice in her glass clinks as her feet shift rather unintentionally. Our father begins to move towards her, and when he sees us looking at him, he cracks a big smile, a smile that reminds me of Ron's laugh. He veers towards us.

"But really, in the end…"

*bought one because she told me to. So I'm eating the cheese pastry slowly, in the square, surrounded by hunters and rifles and the smell of dead game, and they're passing me the wine.*

Our father is in front of us, hunkering down on one knee. "...offensive to live with so little money." He's touching your hair, Anna, and taking my hand, and asking us how we're doing. Fine, we say. Why don't you "fun for a while, but not all that practical to be romantic forever, now is it?" come over here and say hello to Mr. Milne.

Then we're walking past Vicki and she's saying "Luthier, huh? My, but it's a beautiful word though," and she's tilting her glass back and slurping at the ice cubes in her empty tumbler while watching her husband rest a hand on the waist of Mrs. Milne's polyester dress.

*They're watching me loving eating this pastry and they're laughing. I offer them some and they shake their heads, saying* bon appétit bon appétit *and so I split it into a million pieces and*

*postcard*

I'm on his shoulders and he's walking down through maple trees in the ravine behind the school you and I went to, shuffling the first fallen leaves away with his feet. There are colours dripping in great gobs off delicate branches above me, bouncing past my wide eyes with each of his steps. You're running ahead of us because you're older, too big to be on his shoulders, but only just. We get to the bottom, and he's pulling me high overhead and setting me down, letting us run through the deep carpet of leaves like puppies. We tear recklessly through the muck, at once completely absorbed and yet easily wrenched out of that absorption by a flash of luminescence, or a scent. He's standing by silently, staring up at the thinning canopy, or off down the ravine, as if it reminds him of somewhere he doesn't want to say.

He's standing there, oblivious to our antics, staring up at the yellows, oranges and reds saturating the sky, and you're running great big circles around him and I'm standing belly-button deep in a sea of decomposing leaves, staring up at him, thinking, "Who are you? What are you doing here? With us?"

*they're all smiling as they chew. I hear a soft, familiar scraping sound. I look up and see a man standing in a window holding a small plane. In the window next to him hang three violins and a*

A bicycle. A virgin. He takes the training wheels off and I try and try and don't get it, but then he gives me a good shove, strong enough so that it's easier for me to keep my balance and suddenly it's there, I'm riding the bike. He runs alongside me for a while. The wind on my face is something else. I still remember how it felt, the wind and hearing him laughing all that way behind me, realizing that I was doing this on my own, that he'd stopped running, was no longer beside me. That I was riding. Away from him.

*cello, in various stages of completion. He bends and scrapes, bends and scrapes. Bends and scrapes. The man next to me is telling me where all the good rabbits are. It's on your way out of town, he's saying, pointing with a finger caked in dried blood, just over that hill there.*

*postcard*

**Avranches:** *An old woman discovers me in her barn, after dark. She comes over and shakes me, smiles and hands me a milk jug, empty. It's good that you're here, I need help tonight, she says, and points me to a goat. Afterwards, she feeds me apples and dough baked in a pan and pulls the straw out of my hair. I smell like goats and wood smoke all evening, a new burst of perfume drifting up to my nose with each movement I make. Now, she says, handing me a blanket, go to sleep, and remember. Dream, you mean? I ask her. No, she says, remember.*

Audio tape. The luthier.

*"I was on the bus coming back from buying some glue one day and I passed a young girl near the theatre. You know, the one across from the drugstore? Well, I looked at her and wondered about her — about where she lived, how old she was, what she was doing, what grade she was in — and when I was half a block past her, I realized it was Sophia. I'd looked at her for a good fifteen seconds and not recognized her." A cough. A clearing of the throat. A few seconds of awkward silence before a fumble. The machine is turned off.*

I am eight. Our eyes lock, him on the bus and me on the street and he stares back at me in complete and total confusion, *irrecognition*, and I know then that he'll do it, but don't want to believe it.

He comes home early the next day. I look up at him from my book. He looks at me. Does not say anything, does not even open his mouth. Turns and goes up the stairs, where I hear him pulling something heavy out of the hallway closet. His steps move across the ceiling into the bedroom, the mattress breathes a loud sigh and there is a long silence. I sit in front of my homework, staring at a suspended point in space for I don't know how long. You were at softball practice.

Eventually I look up, blink and find myself on the back step of the house and he's beside me. He's telling me why he's doing what he's doing, and I'm receiving it in raindrops, phrases spattering all around me, forming rivulets and flowing away from me.

*An imagined conversation. The luthier. And me. In the living room. He rifles through a pile of papers and oversized books and comes back, carrying an atlas, to where I'm sitting. He opens it to one of the pages at the beginning, where there is a map of the world. And he circles his finger*

*postcard*

*Met at*
                *last year*
      *friends of*
                        *involved*
                                    *(shouldn't be, I know, but…)*
*see her every afternoon*
*I want to*        *love her freely*
                                      *(I'm sorry)*
*leaving*
      *might as well tell you everything*
                              *pregnant*
*She loves me*

And then he's gone, dragging his suitcase behind him — it gets stuck in the door. Wrestling.

*Tell your mother*

*please*

---

*in the air above it all. "I'm from here," he says, with three fingers on the map, each a continent apart: Tehran, Paris, Toronto. "I was born here." He lifts his fingers off Paris and Toronto. "My family lives here." He takes his finger off Tehran and places it on Paris. "I grew older*

*postcard and other stories*

The last time I saw him. 1977.

here." He leaves his finger on Paris, but places another on Toronto, tapping. "And I returned to here." He places all his fingers on Tehran. He looks up at me and shrugs. "That's who I am." After a while, "Show me where you were."

*postcard*

A sighting. I'm walking back from my friend's place. I'm, oh, fourteen, fifteen. I'm walking down the street, a side street, I can't remember which, and I'm walking towards Roncesvalles, it's not far now. And just when I'm about there, he walks past. He's about fifteen feet away, and he's with her, whom I've never met, and they're not talking, they're just walking. I'm thinking they must live close by, because they have that air about them that says they have purpose, not that they're just out for a stroll in a neighbourhood they don't frequent all that often. They look like they're on their way to buy toothpaste, or a loaf of rye, something. And I'm about to call out, to say, "Hey, it's good to see you," and then he looks over his shoulder, turns his head right past me and back again and keeps walking.

And I'm still thinking I'll call out and say something — I'm tailing them while I'm trying to get up the courage — and then I realize that I'm trying to get up the courage and it's a blow to realize that you're scared of your father, that you feel like you can't even go up to him and say hello and not because of anything you've ever done wrong. Not like anything's your fault. I stop then, halfway across an intersection, looking after him, as he walks with her, and then someone bumps into me and a car horn honks and the person who bumped into me tells me that I'm not very smart but I don't care because through the weft of other people on the sidewalk I just saw him put his arm around her in a very fragile way and I'm trying to absorb something I never expected to see.

*"When you were gone?"*
*"No," he says, "With the postcards."*

In the park one night. The one with the tennis courts, which I like because I love the *punck* of tennis balls bouncing, and because it's an unusually shaped park. Everything about it is a little off-kilter, angular, somehow. We're on the swings, you and I, and I'm somewhere between six and eight, so let's call it seven, and you must be nine, and our mother has just told us that she miscarried before she had either one of us. We're there swinging, and my friend Cathy shows up and hops on one of the swings too and then we're all swinging and it's about seven o'clock and we have to be home for dinner soon. The sky's all dark and eerie. But we're swinging. And I tell Cathy that our mother almost had a baby a few years before she had you, but that the baby died. And it occurs to me, while we're swinging and talking, that if she hadn't miscarried, we'd have (it was a boy) a brother, and you'd be in the middle and I'd still be the youngest. That there is a whole different plane that exists, one which hovers slightly above us, above the ground that we have our pre-adolescent feet bolted to. What might have been. Teasing.

I tell Cathy this and she looks at me like I'm a freak. You just keep swinging, not saying anything. And the horizon is suddenly no longer black. There's some kind of green, ghoulish glow and we all look at it and slowly stop swinging. There's no one else around. No one in their front yards, no one walking their dog. Not even some stranger peering around a dilapidated screen door, telling us to get home. The air is completely still. Not even birds are chirping. No dogs barking. Nothing is moving. And we all look at each other and think holy shit. We jump off the swings and start running. We're small and can't run very fast, but we're running. And we get about half a block and the rain comes. Sweeping, violent sheets of it. And wind. It takes about half a second before we're soaked and we're still running until we realize that there really isn't much point. We can't decide what to do then because we're scared — the wind is ripping branches off trees at that point, and it's hailing golf balls, you get a cut on your cheek from one — but we're laughing.

"Oh." *I look at the map for a moment and then draw a long sweeping line down from London, curving across the body of Europe — France, the Rhine, Prague — straightening out down*

*postcard*

We get to Cathy's house and you and I keep going because Cathy's mom yells at Cathy to get inside and for us to get the hell home and we have half a mile to go, so we're running again and it's 7:30 on a July night and it feels like midnight. Pitch black. We're holding hands and running and we finally get home. And there's a hailstone the size of a baseball in our driveway. We grab it and take it inside and put it in the freezer.

I remember just being happy to be alive. That feeling of gratefulness and exhilaration that I wasn't the baby who died, and neither were you. That I was still on the same plane as you, and Cathy, and Mom and Dad.

The hail sat in the freezer for a long time, until it evaporated into a piece of ice the size of an ice cube. As though it was the only thing that remained of the four of us together.

*towards Italy and then a sharp turn east — Istanbul, the Black Sea, a Russian border, the Persian Gulf — and end with my finger in mid-air, poised over a wedge of water between Asia and Africa.*

You're in the car, both of you. She's driving you to your softball game. I'm sick, at home. It's raining out, grey. She doesn't want me playing in that weather, even though my fever's only slight. The field isn't far, but she wants to drive you. You're wearing your shiny red team shirt with "Ackland's Pharmacy" written in white letters that used to stick to my fingers when I touched them, in a curve across the back. You're number 17. You had to flip a coin with Lynn Hadley to get that number, because she wanted it too. You won the toss. You got number 17.

You're ten, older than me by a year and a half. Our mother's driving you down Sorauren and the rain's coming down really hard. Most of the time it doesn't feel like you're older. It's raining so hard that she doesn't see the stop sign. Most of the time it feels like we're friends, even when your other friends are around. A big garbage truck comes through the intersection. I remember you always as ten years old, grinning, like you did at me when you got into the car in the driveway that afternoon. Hits the car. Pushes your side of the car up against her and crushes you between her and the frame. Pinching me and telling me that I was OK. There is blood and dissolved you everywhere. "You're really OK," you'd say. And I always felt that I was, when you said that. And then you're gone. And our lives become even more splintered.

Two weeks later, our mother is sitting at the kitchen table with a cup of tea, looking out of the window at the rain. And she asks out loud, "Why was I driving her to a softball game in a downpour?"

We don't know.

*"Where did you find out?"*
*I point to central Iran. Shiraz. He smiles.*

*postcard*

An audio tape again. Played over and over in my room after the Super 8 film broke. Volume as low as possible.
"*Describe a sunrise,*" I say.
"*A sunrise is the feeling of blood slowly spreading across cold skin.*"
*(He hums quietly.)*
"*Describe leaves,*" I say.
"*Oh, that's hard…. Leaves are like… small flashes of light when your eyes are closed.*" *(A shuffle in the background.)*
"*Mmmm.*"
"*Describe a silhouette.*"
"*A whisper. A small breath. It's not meant to be felt…*" *(pause)* "*but it raises the tiny hairs on your arms as it passes over you.*"

"*I fainted at Persepolis.*"
*He laughs and says,* "*Ah, well, that must mean good luck.*" *He traces around my finger.*

1980. A shaft of light on my bed, like someone flicked the switch on a spotlight. There's a shadow stamping towards me and then I'm out of bed, being dragged by the arm into the bathroom. Our mother's slamming the door, flicking the light on, all the white tile blinding. She's red, she's crying. She's frantic. You died a few days ago, and the funeral was yesterday. She's got the medicine cabinet open and she's sweeping all the pills into a plastic bag, hyperventilating. Now the light's off again and we're in my room. "Get dressed," she's saying. And then she closes my door and stands in the hallway.

I get dressed and sit on the bed and when she opens the door a few moments later, she's looking at me and saying, "Let's go." Now the house is quiet.

We're driving, we're driving then, and I'm in the back seat, squinting at the streetlights in the rain, and she's got the windshield wipers going on doublespeed and we're driving past your school, the one I was just about to start going to, Anna. We're driving past the softball diamond, and we're going up Dundas and then Scarlett and then Weston Road. And just before we get to the highway, she goes down a side street and we're at the back of a cemetery.

She gets out of the car, grabs the bag with the pills and opens the back door, waiting for me to get out. It's pouring rain, and in the race out of the house, both of us forgot our raincoats. Come on, she says, standing there, already soaked, her hair plastered against both cheeks. I shunt myself across the seat, step out into the mud. It's cold.

*I draw a line northwest to Istanbul, tap my finger on it. He looks up at me with raised eyebrows.*

*postcard*

We walk to your grave — it's all still freshly mounded — and when we're there she kneels in the dirt, Anna, and I think she's going to cry, but she's more composed than I've ever seen her. Her face is set, determined.

She's opening the bag and pointing into it. She's telling me to open all of the pill bottles and pour the pills into her hand. I'm frozen. I can't move. DO IT she's yelling, so I put my knees in the dirt and I'm rifling through the bag, giving her laxatives and antacids and lithium and valium and baby aspirin. Her hand's out and it's shaking and she's shoving everything in her mouth and she's got nothing to swallow with but she keeps going anyway and it's really difficult for me to tell if her face is wet from the rain or because she's hysterical. She's quiet, just pushing air through her nose every few seconds, her cheeks puffed out with the pills and she's trying to swallow. Now she's squeezing her eyes shut and leaning over, whimpering, banging her head on her fists, in the mud. And I get up and stand over her, put my small hand on her back and she stops. She stops. She just breathes for a minute. She stands up, spits the pills into her hand, flings them on the grave, spits more out, flings again. And then she leans over, spitting slowly, letting saliva just drip from her mouth while she wails. She straightens up after a minute and she just stands there with her fists clenched for an hour or so while it keeps on raining and I watch the pills dissolve on that freshly mounded soil, streaks of pink and blue training through it like the mascara on her face. And then I take her hand and I tell her I'm cold and we turn away from the grave and we're walking back towards the car and we're going home.

*"You went back?"*

A cold evening. 1986. Our mother is somewhere else tonight. I don't know where. I've come to the darkest place I could find in the city, scoped it out weeks beforehand, because this is something I've really wanted to see. A meteor shower. And here I am, with three sweaters and a hat and wool gloves, lying on ground just about to harden into winter. I'm just lying there, thinking to myself — things I can't remember — and suddenly you're there.

We're lying on our backs in a big field, looking up at a meteor shower.
"*There's one — did you see it?*" you say.
"Yeah — it's still there — see? Oh… it's gone."
Silence.
"They remind me of you."
"*What do?*"
"The meteors."
"*Why?*"
"Because they flash past everything — they don't stay as long as you want them to." Just the sort of clichéd thing a seventeen-year-old would say. I don't know any better, Anna, but I mean it.

The meteors are kind of like slow-motion fireworks; small, intermittent, random flashes, but if you were to put them all together, their brightness, their fire, their streaks across the whole length of the sky would make it as bright as daylight.

"*I don't ever remember seeing meteors,*" you say.
"No? I thought we saw lots, when we were growing up."
"*Shooting stars, yeah, but not meteors.*"
"They're the same thing."

*I look at him and nod.*
"*To find him?*"

*postcard*

You say the best thing in the world then, Anna. You say: *"Does that mean we get to wish every time?"* You're asking me a question, Anna, exactly how I remember you would ask it.

And I'm seventeen, and I can't think of anything to wish for because, even though all the things in my life aren't smooth and clearly defined (nor have I realized yet that they never will be), you're there.

*I nod.*
"And you didn't?"

The next day, we're driving downtown, our mother and I. The sky is big, clouds like oil paint, textured and smooth at the same time. I'm in the back seat, where I always have to sit, since the accident, and you're beside me and we're listening to the Filipino Radio Hour and you're giggling at the splashes of English — the phone numbers, street addresses, colloquialisms — that pepper a language we don't understand. I'm not laughing. I'm just imagining you. I'm looking out the window at the clouds. You're dead, but I can feel you beside me.

*I squint and waggle my head sideways.*

*postcard*

**Paris:** *I've heard that at the end of your life, your mind turns not so much toward a linear recap of events, but more a drifting in and out of the most mundane moments, where your sense of time bends from the linear into something more circular. It's a way to quietly absorb the realization that the moment of your death occurs while you're still breathing/living.*

*I don't think that happens with suicide.*

A dream.

"Promise me something," he says. And I'm still naïve enough — no, desperate enough (because he only just started disappointing me then, Anna) — to say OK without asking what, because I remember what he was like when you were around, and how much easier it was to admire him then, and I haven't entirely let go of that yet.

"Promise me, Anna, that you'll never forget me the way I was, when you were alive," he says — to me, Anna, to me. "Promise me you'll always see me that way."

I stare at him. I'm ten. I have no concept of guilt, or parenthood, or the magnitude of death. He's gone, you're dead, but the size of both those things hasn't hit yet. I can do that, I think. Of course I can do that. It's all I want right now.

I smile and don't say anything. And then he touches my cheek like he always used to touch yours.

*On New Year's Eve in Peru, you pack a suitcase full of your favourite clothes. You pack it to the brim. You close it. And then, at midnight, you go outside with your suitcase and walk around the block as*

*postcard*

She tells me in the car. We're on a highway and I'm watching her driving, how she twitches her thumbs nervously on the steering wheel as though mosquitoes have landed on them and she's trying to shoo them away without lifting her hands off the wheel, *twitch twitch*.

"How did you fall in love with him?" I ask.

"Who?"

"What do you mean, who? My father, who. Your husband."

"I don't remember. Ex-husband."

"What do you mean?"

"Oh, Sophia, I don't remember the details. I can't tell you if he brought me flowers, or what we had for dinner on our first date."

"Was it something he said, maybe?"

"No, I don't think so." We were quiet for a while. And then she told me. "I did fall in love like that with a man once, but not your father. He was an ornithologist. We met on a trail in the woods somewhere. He asked me what I was doing there, and just as I was telling him that I had no idea, he stopped me, mid-sentence, and cocked his ear, like this, and a bird sang and he said 'Ah... a thrush.'"

"And that was it?"

"That was it."

"When?"

*fast as you can. Faster... then faster than that. You walk around the block with your neighbours, with the rest of your city or village, with people of all ages. You walk around the block with the*

She was quiet.

"Mom...." (panic) "when?"

"Before."

I didn't say anything.

"Before your father left."

I turn and sit back and look straight out of the windshield. After about five minutes, I ask why. She shrugs.

She tells me I don't know anything about love, or the role that trust plays in romance; that when it comes to love, given a chance to tell the truth or lie, men will always lie. They're politicians, skirting the issue or seeking diplomatic solutions, but never admitting exactly what is going on, she says. I look at her, and I start laughing.

I shake my head, incredulous. "So how come you come out all shiny?" I ask.

"Because it's my story, and I'm telling it right now." She smiles, Anna, but she's not joking.

She stares out the windshield, as though what she's just told me is perfectly normal *twitch twitch* and I know that this *twitch twitch* is one of those moments I'll remember forever and I wish that I had more memories of feeling close to her, rather than wondering what the hell she's thinking. *Twitch twitch.* I'm seventeen. I remember how quiet the rest of the car ride was. Just the occasional *shhhh shhhh* of her thumbs on vinyl. *Shhhh shhhh.*

oldest women in town, who grasp the handles of their bags fiercely and waddle quickly, with determination. You walk with young men who swagger and sway. Grannies, children, uncles,

*postcard*

Toronto. The Windsor Arms. The signing of divorce papers. Lunchtime.

I'm skipping a class, lying in the forest just behind the high school you would have gone to before me. I'm on my back, looking up at the trees. Reading *Catcher in the Rye*.

*When she enters the hotel, her toes and fingertips grow icy cold. She checks the bar. He's not there. She asks the maître d' in the dining room if he's arrived yet, but the maître d' shakes his head. She waits at the bar. The prospect of a blank table in front of her is unapproachable. Much better to sit, occupying a small sliver of a long bar, where others are alone too, not waiting at all.*

*She orders a Perrier and wonders how long it will take him to recognize her. They haven't seen each other since the day he left the house, Anna, if you can imagine that.*

*He recognizes her. —You've cut your hair, he says.*

*—Yes, I told you that.*

*—Yes, of course, you did, didn't you? He squeezes into the seat next to her at the bar.*

*He looks at her briefly and then raises a finger to the barkeep and orders a scotch and water. She crosses her legs and leans back in her seat, watching him. He's wearing a dark suit with a crisp, white shirt and as he twists away from her to take his drink from the bar, the shirt tightens against a small bulge of flesh just above his belt... he must be happy, she thinks. Or at least satisfied. He's slightly paler than she remembers him. He turns around to meet her gaze, drink hoisted.*

*—Well, I don't know if we should be toasting...*

*widows, bachelors, all striding, grasping, struggling, laughing. And if you do this, it's said that you will go someplace you've always wanted to go.*

—Of course we should, she says.

—OK, he says, touching her glass.

She hands him the papers after they're led to a table in the dining room. Signed this morning in the kitchen, standing at the counter. He sets the papers aside. —Any problems with it?

—No, no... not at all.

Nice and clean.

He snaps his napkin open and draws it onto his lap when their meals arrive. They do not toast again. He cuts deeply into a steak and asks,

—How's Sophia?

—Fine. You should see her sometime.

—Mmm...

—She's your daughter.

He looks up. —Look, it's just... it's not a good time. It's too complicated to explain. He pushes a piece of steak into his mouth.

—You haven't seen her in six years.

He stops chewing, stares back at her. Our father, Anna.

At dessert, he asks her if she'll get remarried. She laughs and stirs some sugar into a cup of tea.

—It's not the first thing on my mind right now, she says. —And you? He shrugs. —Sure I will, maybe... I don't know.

We got a postcard from him, from Shiraz, when I was nineteen. A couple of years later, I went to

*postcard*

*—Are you still with her?*

*—No.*

*—What happened?*

*He shrugs again. He looks directly at her. —It was too much.*

*She raises her eyebrows. —And?*

*—And I'm with someone else now. She's… His eyes flick away. —She's a student. He looks directly at her again.*

*—Of? she asks, bemused.*

*—Nothing in particular.*

*—A student?*

*He says nothing, does nothing.*

*After that conversation, she takes the ferry to Toronto Island and rides it back and forth until she's certain the ground beneath her feet will not collapse, that it's firm, solid. She needs to be sure of that.*

*Iran, by way of Europe, to look for him. Foolish girl.*

**Prague:** *I wanted our legacies to be visceral, filled with stories that defined us, or which at least contained defining moments, like the Inuit woman who cut strips of flesh from her own forearm to feed her child when the plane that came to rescue her crashed in the bush. And I wanted our parents to give it to me, to present it to me like they would a birthday gift, all wrapped up in mystery, a reading between the lines of history, a place where embellishment finds a home.*

*postcard*

*Foolish, foolish girl.*

Another dream. The one I had last night, on the cusp of a new millennium. *I was watching from behind a window. At first I was just watching the wind blowing up on a distant hill, in trees turning colour, thinking that it felt like it was going to snow. I was behind glass, but I could hear the wind as though I was on the other side of it. And it was a turning-winter wind — the kind of wind that sounds like snow coming, simply because it no longer has so many leaves to push through. The sound of austerity.*

*And into the picture, in the lower right-hand corner of the window, crept our mother. She was a tiny figure and she wore a shiny red slicker like Little Red Riding Hood wore in that book we had growing up. And she was shunted over, her face made invisible by the hood. She shuffled into centre frame and in retrospect, I do not know how I knew it was her, I just had that sensibility that only occurs in dreams where even when you cannot possibly know who a character is, you feel absolutely certain that you do. She stood, her back to me now, staring out at the trees as I did, her crimson hood pointing prominently towards the sky, matched on either side by the yellows and oranges of errant leaves. She simply stood. And I felt like knocking on the pane of glass, but I didn't. I could feel myself thinking that I ought to, that I ought to bang it and bang it as hard as I could, bang it until it shattered so that we might have one less thing between us. But I didn't. And when she finally turned, I expected something out of a Hollywood script; I expected either a skull to appear tucked in the hood, or for it to be entirely empty, and in shrinking back from it, I missed it. I missed what was inside. She turned back quickly. I could hear words building up somewhere, and I cocked an ear to listen.*

In the Sultanahmet, in the alleyways between mosques and palaces and teahouses, I'm surrounded by water — the Sea of Marmara that stretches south of the city like an azure plain, the Bosporus cutting the city and the world in half, Europe, Asia, the bow of a freighter silently and largely looming into view, the sound of slapping liquid, waves against its hull, sliding between you and another continent a stone's throw away. The landscape above it scattered with the minarets of a dozen mosques, each releasing their own call to prayer, each briefly competing with the others for the air and ears, one fading out after another until only a solitary wail remains — the staticky howl for Allah drifting across the water quickly in the breeze that always seems to blow on the Golden Horn. I sit in an alleyway at a small table with a red-checkered tablecloth and I order a bowl of lentil soup, then eggplant with yogurt and garlic. The breeze is pushing through my hair. I unwrap a package of postcards that I've just bought.

*postcard*

*I felt then as if I was pulling myself back quickly, smoothly, almost externally, like something was waking me up to protect me from what I might hear. I literally opened my eyes* moving, pulling myself backwards across the bed. I was at its upper corner, sheets tossed off the edge, suddenly and vertically crouched in a fetal position.

*The sound of a chair scraping draws my attention back to the alleyway.*

*Romance.*

A man stands at my table, holding the chair in front of me, gesturing. His hand sweeps over the entire alleyway filled with tables and he shrugs — all of the tables are taken. "Of course, of course," I say and motion for him to sit down. As he does, he leans over and gently presses his finger to his lips and then to mine. I pull back for an instant, but his eyes are trying to tell me something, something he can't actually say out loud. He orders from the waiter, who seems to have seen him maybe just once before, by pointing at various dishes on the customers' tables. We eat, and our ears are filled with other people's conversations. I understand very little of what is spoken and can't decide if he understands either. I keep silent. I'm intrigued, Anna, so very intrigued, and try to sneak glances at him as he eats, trying not to stare. I suspect, though I don't know why, that he doesn't live here. When I look away, he keeps his gaze on me, retribution for my curiosity, I think, and when I look back, he's smiling shyly, still staring at me, strongly now. Ah, he cannot speak. The din of conversation fades and our eyes are flitting back and forth from each other. Our plates are taken away and two small tulip-shaped glasses of tea and a large bowl mounded with sugar cubes are put in front of us. He takes a sugar cube, placing it between his teeth, raises his glass to his lips and quietly sucks the tea through the sugar cube with pursed lips. Oh, if you could see it. He blinks slowly and looks up at me as I stir sugar into my glass. The waiter places a saucer with a piece of baklava on it in front of him. I sip my tea, rearrange my gaze, and he leans towards me with something in his hand. I lean forward and wrap my lips gently around the honey-soaked baklava, saliva collecting under my tongue. I slowly bite down, pull back and let it dissolve in my mouth for a moment before closing my eyes and chewing. He licks his fingers, delicately, watching me.

*postcard*

*Marriage.*

*He takes my hand as we leave the noise of other people's conversations and leads me to an apartment a few blocks away. As we climb a dark set of spiral stairs, one behind the other, he crouches so that he can still hold my hand. He opens the door into a large room with pillars, a terrace lit by the moon splayed beyond a wall of paned glass. He shuts the door, slowly pushes me against it and leans into me, kissing me softly, unerringly, for a long time. He drops the keys as his hand relaxes and I pull him gently closer, still kissing the first long kiss. Nervousness ripples along my limbs, and when he unclenches my fists for me, kissing each of my fingers as he unravels them, the tingling in my stomach spreads over my whole body and I can no longer hear anything, not even the sound of his breathing. I tilt my head back as he kisses my neck. The moonlight has faded and the room is completely dark. A sudden patter of rain on glass fills the room. Water. I close my eyes.*

Mild irritation.

*A distended wail of the pre-dawn call to prayer pulls me out of sleep. I lie still, listening for his breath. He's warm, exhausted. I feel as though I ought to leave, but don't want to. After half an hour of thinking about it, I'm fully awake and decide to go. I rise from the bed and look onto the terrace. The sky is brightening. I lean over and gather my clothes, slipping them on quickly. Tempted to give him one last long kiss. Instead, I lean over him and inhale, for one long minute. Tiptoe to the door, and slip out. A garbage truck clamours by when I step onto the street. The sun has risen. I walk slowly back to my room, fifteen minutes away, under the monstrous, magnificent layered domes of the Hagia Sofia.*

~

*He speaks first. What is your name? he writes on a piece of paper he has taken from a table by the bed. I move to take the pen from his hand, but he pulls it back out of my reach. He presses his fingers to my lips, then makes a waving motion, releasing my name from my mouth. "Sophia," I say. I smile, covering my mouth at the sound of my voice. He laughs, silently. This is the third morning we've woken up together, the fourth morning since we met. I've learned to sleep through the day's first call to prayer, but am usually roused a few minutes later by the shimmering of his hand over my skin. I point to the piece of paper and then to him. "What's your name?" I ask aloud, more confident with my voice. He lies back on the bed and draws letters in the air.*

*postcard*

**Pregnant.**

e  t  h  a  n

## Revival.

He stretches over to a table by the bed, turns back to me and hands me his wallet. He flaps his hand at me, telling me to open it. He props himself up on an elbow while he watches me. His bag, packed, lies across the room. I squirm, rearranging myself so that it's out of view. I lie naked on my stomach and open the wallet uneasily, looking at him as I do. He grins and waves his hand at me again. Go on... Two pieces of ID lie under clear plastic. A birth certificate for Lemieux, Ethan Georges, born in Baltimore, 1966. I look up at him, placing him with this new information. "American," I say. He shakes his head and points to the other piece of identification, which has his photo on it. I hold the photo up to his face, smiling, then squint at the printing. Lemieux, Ethan Georges, 11 rue Desrosiers, Paris. Of course. As I reach down into my pile of clothes for my passport, I laugh at the idea of a French lover. I toss him the passport and turn on my side. I catch a glimpse of his bag again and inch up on the bed so that my body hides it from view. He flips the passport open, smiles and looks at me when he sees the photo, then slowly starts turning through the pages, looking at the stamps. He looks up at me, amused, knowing there's a story. He shrugs, pointing to the passport. I take it from him, turn to the third page and begin to tell him: "I'm from Canada." He moves closer to me. "Je parle français," I say, and continue my story in French as he smiles, listening and playing with a strand of my hair. Eventually I stop, my monologue fizzling out as I realize I'm being indulgent with words, filling air that has been gloriously silent for the past four days. His hand, on the back of my knee, pulls my leg gently forward and he runs his fingers over my thigh. He stops suddenly, leaning back to grab the pen from the table again, writing a question on the piece of paper. Que faîtes-vous? He pushes the note to me. What do you do? I laugh, finding it charming that he uses the "vous" form. Je me souviens, I write back, Et <u>toi</u>? He considers for a moment, and writes something, but before I can read it, he pulls me slowly towards him and kisses me, moving his hand to my inner thigh, into swollen folds of skin. I close my eyes and feel my limbs lengthen and all sound is blocked from my ears except the deep hum of blood running through my core. I slowly push him onto his back, my fingers tracing the humps and valleys of each of his ribs, the flattened swirl of hair at his belly button, the darkness of his inner thighs, muscles twitching, lengthening, stiffening.

We return to the restaurant where we met, sitting outside in the alleyway again, completely unconcerned that a very slight, unexpected mist has begun to fall. The waiter recognizes us and with a gracious smile brings us exactly what we ordered four nights ago. We stare and smile at each other as we eat. He teaches me how to suck tea through a sugar cube. I push baklava slowly into his mouth, he bites down, I lick my fingers, watching him. He reaches over and pushes stray hair behind my ear and lets his hand rest on my cheek, stroking my damp eyebrow. He gets up and goes inside the restaurant and I watch him, moving inside, offering a quick profile as he looks for the waiter. I push my chair back quietly and get up. I leave some money stuck under the sugar-cube bowl, more than enough to pay for dinner. And then I walk quickly down the alleyway, not looking back. It's the strangest feeling in the world, Anna, like I cut myself but won't let myself look at the wound because I'm afraid it might not be as deep as I think. As though its size, its smallness, might not warrant its throbbing. I turn a corner and catch a view of the water. I put my hands in the pockets of my jeans. I touch paper. Something he has hidden for me, and let me find.

What is your name?
Que faîtes-vous?
Je me souviens. Et <u>toi</u>?
Je vis.

I close my eyes, trying to memorize his face.

*postcard*

*Pregnant.*

Iran. Ochres murmur in the mountains; green shrieks on her plains; turquoise calms, repeating the colour of her cloudless skies, in tiles on minarets. Hand-painted. From afar, perfection. Up close, uneven strokes, the jerk of a painter's hand reveals their fallibility. The whole country seems to sleep outside, on rooftops, as if in reverence to the lack of rain. At dawn, the muezzin's call and a hot, sandy wind and all Iran is a view of bedsheets rippling over mattresses and frames, empty by sunrise.
Eventually, a stone's throw away from Shiraz. Persepolis. I wander through a maze of pillar bases, through gates of stone carved into bulls, birds, lions. An Iranian family strolls in front of me with the sort of resignation that comes with the obligations one feels at famous monuments, just as I would at Niagara Falls. Their child sees a camel carved into grey stone, a bas-relief at eye-level to him. I stand in the whiteness of the sun, the stone, the desert, millennia of mistakes we call history. I close my eyes and try to find you. A sad, lamentful song drifts out from under a willow tree nearby, its singer hidden by the tree's boughs. An anonymous series of notes. The pillars tumble before me like a set of pickup sticks. My head hits the ground. The sun dazzles me black.
In the doctor's office, they tell me I'm pregnant. They ask me where the father is and I say he's not with me right now. They nod and don't ask any other questions. The doctor takes my hand and presses some ginger candies into it, telling me to eat them if I feel nauseous. Then she smiles at me, runs her hand over my head and walks out the door.
Later, I watch a grandmother at the entrance to a bazaar, hiking her chador over her head as she passes a handful of coins to a candy vendor, buying a treat for a grandson, maybe, his smile already imagined. A man hunched over, carrying a load of sticks on his back, for fire, for food. The air feels different — light, and tender. The sky looks different.

*Affair.*

The Mayans believed that when the gods created us, they gave us the power to see past the horizon. For a split second, at the very beginning of our history, of our consciousness, they granted us all possibilities. And then they threw dust into our eyes, made us aware of the impossible. They made us mortal, flawed.

*postcard*

*Unravelling.*

A phone call placed from Shiraz.

—Marabah. You had a guest at your apartment, about two months ago. A Frenchman. Ethan. Do you know where he went?
(One moment please...
Hello? He left a note. He will be here again on the seventeenth...)
—Please tell him that I need to see him. Please tell him to meet me at the restaurant on the eighteenth at... two o'clock. Teşekkür.
(You're welcome. But which restaurant? What is your name?)
—Sophia. The one in the alley, but he'll know both of those things.

## Suspicion.

The eighteenth. I stand at the entrance to the alleyway, half an hour early. The Bosporus shines on the horizon, rippling in a gusty breeze from Asia. I lean against the brick wall of one of the restaurants at the edge of the alley. The place where Ethan and I met is further down, but I

*postcard*

*Infuriation.*

don't want to go there just yet. I leave the alley and walk towards the water. I pass under domes and minarets stretching into an air that still reverberates from the muezzins' wails from nearly an hour ago. The water steadies me. I sit down at the docks at Sirkeci, watching men fishing

*postcard and other stories*

*Accusation.*

*off the bridges stacked through the waterways of Istanbul like dominoes. I watch men in booths*

*postcard*

*Departure.*

making lahmacun, *spreading a spicy lamb paste over thin sheets of bread and rolling them around*

*Confusion.*










bunches of cilantro. I watch boats rumble through the water, churning up flotsam and foam.

*postcard*

*Accident.*

*I'm not sure what I expect from him, Anna.*

*Death.*

*Nothing, I think, but that he should know.*

*postcard*

***postcard:*** On a coast, limbs of cypress, arced inland. Stretching away from water, not towards it, like we've always been told. Wind stronger than water. Paper scissors rock. Wood bent by air.

*Impermanence.*

Fog descends at night like snow, falling through the air diagonally, down from the light of lampposts. A man walking ahead of me disappears in it, then mysteriously, inexplicably, reappears a moment later, behind me. At the beach in the morning, a massive white break, spray flailing in the wind, a grey fog bank hovering eerily, inches above my head. Surfers burst through the fog.

*postcard*

Nothing propelling towards honesty.

Say one night you take a small gun, hold it against your temple and pull the trigger.

*postcard*

**Napoli:** *I pass a restaurant where a woman is serving an Ethiopian dish: a white globe lying atop a thick, dark stew of shredded chicken. The man she's serving says, "Is that an egg? I didn't order an egg…" And she replies: "But sir, the mother and the child. We never separate the two."*

I'm sitting in our mother's room. There's no colour left. The walls are empty, the venetian blinds open. The floor is bare, except for two faded striped mattresses sitting atop rickety metal legs that rest gingerly on the hardwood. The room is quiet, but I can sense it shifting, creaking, adjusting to her absence. She was here, sleeping, not so long ago.

There's a distant noise, the distinct, soft clunk of mail coming through the slot. After a moment, I push myself up from the floor and stumble down the stairs. A foot from the door, on the floor, lies a postcard. Addressed to our mother. I pick it up.

Shiraz.

A market scene. Piles of vividly coloured spices, brass pans hanging from hooks, coppersmiths banging out their craft on the stoops of their shops, darkly clothed men and women crowding an alleyway, a side of lamb suspended in a doorway. Dust rising.

My hand starts to shake as I begin to read.

*In Valencia there's a law that says you can pick as many oranges as you like, from as many trees as you like, but they must be eaten under their trees.*

*postcard*

**Shiraz:** *Remember the morning we woke up and decided to spend the day doing things we'd never done before? We drove to the coast through towns we'd never seen, rented a skiff and fished in Lake Ontario... we didn't catch a thing, but bought some fresh smelt when we got back to shore, which neither of us had ever had. We ate collard greens. Made love on a deserted beach at sunset and found sand in all our crevices for days afterwards. I've taken part of you with me.*

*Richard*

This is how she did it. She left the blue house near Roncesvalles one dusky summer evening, and walked a distance greater than she normally would to a local movie house, otherwise known as *a repertory cinema*, where The Philadelphia Story was playing. She purchased a *ticket*, went in, sat about two-thirds of the way back from the *stage* and *screen*, and settled in. She did not remove the *light, stiff, three-quarter-length, wide-collared, big-buttoned spring jacket* she was wearing. She did not buy popcorn, or a drink. She merely *sat*.

She sat most of the way through the movie, until the *bathhouse* scene, when Cary Grant destroys Katharine Hepburn's confident perception of herself in one fell swoop.

*In the sun, in a breeze, on a beach not far from where the ferry to Italy is docked, a child with long black hair approaches me and asks a question in Turkish.*

*postcard*

*Hepburn:* You seem quite contemptuous of me all of a sudden.
*Grant:* No, Red, not of you, never of you.
He says she could be the finest woman on this earth, but that something inside of her — *her blank intolerance* — is what he finds contemptuous.
Says she'll never be first class until she gives up her *inner divinity*, caves to some frailty, allows herself — and others — a mistake now and then.
She bristles. If he says another word she'll...
I'm through, Red, he replies. For the moment I've had my say.

*And then he tips his drink down his throat.*

According to a handful of people sitting behind her, our mother stood up then, pulled a small, ivory-handled pistol from her handbag and shot herself in the right temple.

She'd pinned a note to her chest, a quote from Turgenev. Pinned it under her buttoned-up jacket, so that when the paramedics came, it was the first thing they would find, looking for her heartbeat.

*I could not simplify myself.*

It (suicide, I mean) seems so random, until you discover details like this.

*I recognize a couple of the words that she's saying, but can't piece it all together. I flip through my dictionary, pointing at words. The girl pulls it out of my hands. She searches through it, immediately absorbed — she spends half an hour looking at words, nudging me when she wants to know how to*

*postcard*

The house was empty when I walked back into it. Every meaningful thing gotten rid of, given away or thrown out of her own accord, before she pulled the trigger. The simplicity that we grew up in, resurrected. This was not a spontaneous act.

There was another note, this one not pinned to her chest, this one in an envelope, pushed under the frame of that sepia photo of our great-grandmother — in Prussia — remember that one? The one where she's about six, severe, sitting on a chair beside her brother, more dour than her, and her laced-up leather boots reach her knee but not the ground? Separated by a vase of flowers larger than themselves. That one. Under it was another note. I didn't read it when I found it. I was too shocked by the emptiness of the house. I needed to make sure that it was the only thing she left.

And now I know it is.

*pronounce something.* House, friend, fish, laugh, dog, sand. *As the sun starts to dip lower in the sky, the girl gets up to leave and holds the book back out to me. I take it, look up a word —* gift (hediye) *— and push the book back into her hands. She smiles, blushes, and gives me a hug.*

Sophia,

When I decided to do this, when I HAD HAD ENOUGH of the questions and the guessing and the futility and failure of self-composition, I thought then that I would do it quickly. The first night I thought of it. It was raining, the windows were steamed up and that seemed all so perfect, my not being able to see out.

But it felt like more of a whim than a well thought-out decision, and so I decided not to. I found myself whittling things down — my emotions, my possessions. You might be wondering what happened to them, why the only things that exist of me are the photo of my grandmother on the mantle here, this note, a gun, and a lifeless body.

I met a postulant once, just before I married your father. She was off to a particularly penurious order that required her to give up all of her possessions. She said that photos were the hardest thing she'd had to give away. She said that in the end, she burned them, and wasn't sure if that was right in the eyes of God, but that in doing so she felt she was at least returning them to their ephemeral beginnings.

She was right. Photos were the most difficult part. This was the one I could find no recipient for. Except you. You were always talking about legacy, so here is some of it. I know it's not much of one, especially with you left alone to decipher it all. But I don't even know what to begin to tell you. I'm too tired. I want to step away from all the questions.

At the very worst, I end my life and it all cuts to black. Nothing. That, Sophia, seems so peaceful to me right now. Is there anything wrong with that? To just want some peace?

*M.*

*postcard*

A friend comes over. Listens to my grief for a while. And he tells me that every so often, he receives a parcel from Paris, where his mother lives. The box, always a large one, will arrive, weary from too much salt air and handling. They come randomly. It's always a surprise, Hamid says, and it always holds only one thing. Once she sent his grandfather's hookah, his *ghalian*, a marvel of painted glass and smoky leather tubes that had wrinkles like an accordion. Another time she sent a great old samovar. He says his mother is slowly getting rid of her possessions, preparing herself for death, and he doesn't know what to do. Except thank her.

You had a carpet here once, he says. It looked Persian. It was Egyptian, I say, and I don't know where it is now. Hamid nods his head slowly. It was from my mother's lover. He was from Alexandria, I say. Hamid looks up at me with raised eyebrows. Something he did not know. He nods again, and suppresses a grin, surprised.

He asks me if I'll be all right tonight, in the house alone. I laugh off his concern and say yes. He stands up to leave and stops by the door. He places a hand lightly on my neck. What are you going to do? I shrug. Smile. I don't know.

And then he kisses me. Briefly, but when I look up at him, he kisses me again. And I kiss him.

And while stroking my cheek, he bends down to whisper something in my ear, tells me to be careful not to be caught chasing memories. Of you? I ask. No, he smiles. Of your mother, he says.

*She turns and runs down the beach, thin legs kicking up sand behind her that arcs as high as her head.*

In Persia, he says, we think that life is simple, filled with simple truths that ring out in the most basic of things — a butterfly, a rose, a grain of sand. But we are so complex that we need to remind ourselves of these simplicities. Everything we've invented distracts us, he says, holding a finger up here for emphasis, and prevents us from seeing the truth. We simply exist. *How* is irrelevant. We feel it when we pinch ourselves, we breathe in, we breathe out.

*postcard*

It's nearly four o'clock by the time I reach the alley again.

**Tehran:** *A man holds a chicken between his knees, strokes its neck and back until it seems quite calm, then, with an impossibly thin knife, slowly slits its throat, arcing the neck back to drain the blood quickly from it. The chicken convulses silently in a slow rhythm, a pumping motion. The chicken makes one last, long push forward, and the man looks up and stares at me.*

*postcard*

*I come around the corner and see him turn away.*

IN THE THEATRE. Standing on the spot where she pulled the gun up to her temple and squeezed that little metal crescent that curves so innocently from its body, her body expelling a sighing whimper. Alive. Then dead.

Such a cramped space.

This is not so much chasing a memory, I'm telling myself, as chasing understanding. The theatre owner asks if I want him to stay with me, or to tell me what he remembers. I say no. He tells me if I need him I can find him outside painting the marquee and that I can stay as long as I like, that I can even sit through the double feature tonight, which he recommends. An Italian double bill: Nights of Cabiria/*Le Notti di Cabiria* (a new print, he says, winking, fantastic!), and Everybody's Fine/*Stanno Tutti Bene*. Past and present, he says. I smile.

He walks silently up the aisle and the door swishes then slumps shut. There's that boomy silence that exists only on stages in empty theatres. A silence that wraps warmly around you, comforting, as though this is a place where it's all right to make mistakes. Mistakes, at least, that can be corrected.

I pull a seat down — it creaks and clunks into place — hover a hand across the smooth velour for a moment, then move over a few seats (to one that's not steam-cleaned) and sit, looking at the other seat I pulled down.

*I stop stock-still and watch as his head cranes over his shoulder, over his seat, away from me. He brings his face slowly around and stares at the water I just came from. Hold my breath, but he does not swing his gaze over to me. The expression on his face is chutneyed excitement, confusion, not knowing how much longer he should wait. A waiter comes out of the restaurant.*

*postcard*

I turn and look up at the projection booth. The owner is up there, running the first few feet of film through the projector. He sees me looking at him and leans to open a little window. Do you want to see *The Philadelphia Story*? he asks, I have a copy of it. I turn back and face the screen. Sweat springs up on my forehead.

*What do you…*

*Take a breath. Jesus, breathe!*

*OK. All right.*

I slowly nod my head.

OK, he says. I turn quickly and shout, have to shout so that he will hear me, way up there, *Only the reel with the bathhouse scene*. He stops what he's doing with the projector and leans forward, looking down at me for a moment. OK. He pulls back into the booth and finds the reel. Loads the projector. The lights dim quickly.

I tap my toes nervously. The film jars onto the screen, mid-scene. It's an old print. I look around at the walls of the theatre, watching how they flicker with the changing light of the shots. Jimmy Stewart and Katharine Hepburn have just entered the bathhouse. I feel the clunk of a seat beside me. The theatre owner asks if I mind. I look over at him. No, of course not. Everyone should see a movie in an empty theatre at least once, he says. I nod and he flicks his eyes back to the screen. We are watching and we are watching and Cary Grant comes in and they have their drinks and then Jimmy Stewart leaves and when Cary Grant says that line about human frailty, I start; I swear I can feel the bullet slowly pressing into my heart, Anna, and the owner of the theatre reaches for my hand and takes it in both of his and flattens it and presses it gently between them until the reel is over.

*He moves through the tables, stacking dishes on his arm. A gust pushes his hair into standing tufts, waves through his white, short-sleeved shirt. He stands in front of Ethan, his back to me. He says something. I'm too far away to hear him speak; I only see the motions he makes. Ethan looks straight in front of him as the waiter talks. There is a pause.*

**Skopje:** *In a small cemetery, set on top of a hill, with perhaps a dozen graves, stones set flat into grass, a child lifts his kite into the wind. Behind him a bulldozer's shovel slides neatly into the ground, six feet deep, turns to the side and lets the dirt and rock slip into a pile beside it. A cut of brown bleeding into green. The child's kite turns in the wind, flapping, the sound of distant fireworks, or machine-gun fire.*

*postcard*

Stumbling through darkening streets; I left the theatre just as the Italian double feature was starting, pressed my hand into the theatre owner's again and nearly fled the building, running down Roncesvalles towards light, light, anything shiny and glowing and bursting with neon. Anything with a semblance of life, no matter how artificial — seems oxymoronic, I know, but it's what I need. I'm in front of a late summer midway, surprised as I am every year that the sun sets so early in late August, watching the lights on a Ferris wheel, a real live Ferris wheel, ticker up and down, the flash and ripple of midway lights striating up and around and around and down. I feel as though I was drunk, and that it has passed and I am being drawn languorously out of the dizziness and disorientation of that drunkenness. I wander through the carnival as though in some '70s movie starring Jon Voight, the clickety-clack of game boards and tinny, automated voices of hawkers shouting through megaphones all rotating past as I glide along — it's all so much that I feel as though I am passing through it in the passenger seat of a car, the light and noise so powerful it's washed out, glinting, as though it's reflecting off a windshield and why I find this random light and noise comforting I don't know.

Distortion. Distortion is just a more aggressive form of perspective, Anna.

I start to walk away from it, towards the lake.

My back is to the city. I can still see the midway lights, their reflection only, rippling along the water of the lake, from behind me, through me, in front of me. They're softer now, dulled by the skyscape of the city, towers built not of concrete and steel and glass, but only of harsh light on wavering water. The lake's waves thumping, spreading up on a pebbly shore. A big, fat harvest moon hovering on the horizon. A hundred feet away, sparks from a beach fire fly like fingers out in front of it. Voices, muffled.

*I start to walk towards him. Ethan shrugs and then looks up into the eyes of the waiter.*

*postcard and other stories*

I walk past a yacht club, the lights of the midway and city dim and distant now, and stand at its fence, staring in, listening to the creak of old rope pulling taut against wood and fibreglass as water wavers under hulls.

The wind drops. The voices hush. Gulls are heading for shore and in half a second it's cold. Really cold. It's not the cold from a new wind, just cold air descending fast. And five minutes later a cloud slides over the moon and it starts to rain. It's beautiful. To be in the middle of it and just watch it happen. Like being in a room with two other people when something between them becomes apparent; the way she looks at him, silently, nothing said, but everything immediately clear. A wave spreading over you.

*As he does, pain passes abruptly through him. I stop.*

*postcard*

I've been thinking a great deal lately about how it is that *he* will die.

I discovered a picture of him last night, stuck to the wall, crammed into the small space above the tiled counter and beneath the windowsill in the kitchen, hidden from our mother's purge. It's a picture he let me take, in the ravine, before he left. He's standing against a sky bludgeoned with leaves, visceral red. He's wearing white, his black hair curled against his forehead, his face darkened almost beyond recognition by the flare of the sun, the background blurred by my inexpert hand. He's handsome, glowing. It's how I would choose to remember him, but not usually how I do.

This is how my day begins, waking up to something brilliant and clear and then feeling invincible enough to imagine picking up the phone, dialling seven digits and suppressing the palpitation that I feel when I hear his *hello and when I hear him suck in his breath when I say "It's Sophia." And it suddenly all feels so sad and broken and there's something in me that wants to fix it, that wants to repair it, to take that deep hole that exists in both of us and join them, to take a trowel, load mortar against it and smooth it across that collective gaping wound in one swift movement, have it be filled with something as heavy and impenetrable as concrete, and so I invite him out to lunch, tell him that I came across that picture of him last night, the one with him leaning against a tree in the ravine in the middle of autumn looking all happy and healthy and tanned, and that I'm sorry I hadn't called earlier but that maybe we could catch up over some lunch, some lunch would be good and he agrees. And so we meet at a favourite place of his on Sudbury Street and when I walk in I see he isn't there yet and so I sit at the bar, and the maître d' asks if I'm waiting for someone and I say yes and in comes our father and he scans the room right past me it's been years after all and then back again and catches me the second time and comes over with a big smile. The maître d' says Hello Richard how are you? And our father says Fine this is my — pause — daughter and the maître d' arches an eyebrow and does not say anything for a moment and then says — But I thought... but clamps his mouth shut and I know then that he thought our father only had one daughter, Anna, that one being you, and dead.*

*The waiter puts a hand on Ethan's shoulder and leaves it there for a moment. Then he moves*

And I close my eyes and feel tears on my eyelashes, trying to mentally grab on to something that I can steady myself with, and I imagine him looking away but I swallow then and *we go and sit down and order and drum our fingers on the table while we wait for things to be brought that we can hold and disguise our nervousness with. And he asks me how things are at the house and I tell him about there being nothing there and about the two notes and ask how he heard and he says the police but that he only heard about one note and I say It's the only one you want to know about, trust me. He winces then and asks why I think she did it and I say you can answer that probably just as well as I can which is not well at all but if you really want to know what I think I'd say that it had to do with a fear of living honestly, and by that I mean a fear of being honest to herself and nobody else. He thinks about that and takes a big sip of the scotch that has come and then scans his eyes across and past me, fixing them on a pretty woman on the other side of the room and says, Anna, that he's shocked by our mother's self-centredness at which I laugh and when he looks over at me I smile. And then his lamb comes and my soup comes and we eat in silence except for the occasional obligatory question how is work fine I wish it were more exciting but it's fine what do you mean by exciting oh you know just exciting and so on and so on. I don't ask him about his ambitions, and he doesn't ask me about mine.*

*And quite suddenly I feel as though I'm in a place where all the things I know do not fit snugly into each other, where one truth will not lead into another, even, and that I'm suspended above any sort of definition or attempt at definition, that I own none of it, am responsible for not one note of it, and it feels <u>awe</u>some; beautiful and tragic in that same moment.*

*We skip dessert and we stand outside the restaurant, at a bus stop, a bus that will take me back to the house. We say "Yeah, well...," "I should go," "You have things to do," and "Call me if you need me." A lone bystander listens to our awkwardness, shuffling his feet and pretending to look off at something else, maybe wondering if we're father and daughter and thinking how sad we are. And I look at our father then, Anna, and I remember a quote —  Chekov, I think — that women forgive everything but failure and something collapses in me and I close my eyes again and imagine that our father's already*

*in front of Ethan, blocking him from my gaze, walking towards the restaurant. As he drifts past, Ethan's face bleeds into view. His eyes are closed. I'm trying to inhale but my stomach has seized,*

*postcard*

*walking away, away until I... can't... see... him anymore.* I thought I'd steeled myself against disappointment, but that immunity fails me and I hold my head in my hands. I hold my head in my hands. I wipe the tears from my eyes and lean back and look up at the sky. I feel a hand on my shoulder and the stranger, seeing my distress, hovers beside me, not sure what to do, until finally he leads me to the bus-stop pole and props me up against it, briefly holding me there, like he wants to stay, to offer more, but he can't, so he shuffles back over to the spot where he'd stood while he watched me playing out this whole scene in my head, on my own. The stranger keeps shifting his weight from one foot to the other, casting uneasy but concerned glances at me until the bus comes, which I do not get on, but he does, and I mouth "thank you" to him over and over again as he looks out at me through the glass of the retreating bus, nodding once, ever so slightly.

*will not let me. He pushes his chair back, stands, digs in his pocket. His hair falls over his face, pushed up briefly by the breeze. He leaves some money under the sugar bowl. He moves purely, as*

An image: I'm standing in the doorway to his workshop, but he's looking the other way. The scent hits me first, Anna, the scent which almost knocks me down, transforms me into an eight-year-old again. Sawdust burning on a blade.

"So. One more time, then?"

"Yes."

"Describe expectation."

"That's not fair. That's not the game. You're suppos—"

"I'm trying to help. Describe it."

"Expectation is... that awful feeling in your stomach. Anticipation. Like drinking too much coffee and having it churn through you and feeling unduly anxious, but not being able to do anything about it. Impermanence. The feeling of nothing solid."

"Hmmm..."

"Your turn. You describe it."

"Oh. Um... Expectation is like... hope and... waiting. Like waiting for hope to be turned into something you want... imposing what you want on someone else, and waiting for them to do it. It's being six years old and standing at the door, waiting for your mother to ask you if you'd like her to take you somewhere for ice cream, but never asking her to."

"Hmmmm."

"Describe love."

"Love?"

though we had never met, and never would; he, himself, who would exist whether I was there or not.

*postcard*

"Yes."

"Too daunting."

"Tell me anyway."

Silence. "I don't know. Sometimes it lasts. Sometimes it just ends. It's over. You've used each other up, even though that was not the original intention."

"Hmmmm… I suppose you're right. But what do you want? One word."

"Is it really possible to put what you want into one word?"

"I think so. It's a pretty big word — it encompasses a lot, but I think I know what that word is. Do you?

"No. Do you?"

"Authenticity."

*He's quiet after that, like he's thinking about what I just said, weighing it against his own truth.*

He turns away.

He doesn't *do* anything, doesn't pick up a tool and start carving, doesn't wipe his hands on the bench, or run them through his hair. He just turns away and stands silently looking out his window.

And I want to go over to him and stand behind him and wrap my arms around him and I want him to put his arms on top of mine and squeeze them, and I want to lean my head against his back. But after a while I turn away and walk out of his workshop, looking back once to see him still standing there, looking away, and the whole way home I can smell the sawdust on me, Anna, I smell the wood on me for a long time.

*I turn away.*

**Toronto:** *Do you know the legend of Kasane? It's a Kabuki dance in which two young lovers, Kasane and Yoemon, stroll along a river at night. As they walk, Kasane suddenly turns into a crumpled, ogre-like figure, a mutated reincarnation of a woman Yoemon killed in an earlier life. Yoemon, in a state of shock from recognition, pulls out a blade and tries to kill her: she resists, but Yoemon fights back, stabbing her, and Kasane falls to the stage, dead. Yoemon runs off the stage, escaping along a walkway that dissects the audience. The stage goes black.*

*But after a few moments, once the audience's eyes have adjusted to the dark, a slow, eerie movement can be seen on stage. It's Kasane's hand. She's raising it, pointing it in the direction that Yoemon has gone, and stretching her fingers out, pulling. Yoemon reappears, walking backwards through the audience, drawn by force back to the stage, back to Kasane. Once he reaches her, the story begins again as it did. They meet again, as though for the first time.*

*postcard*

*It's half an hour before sunset. I stumble through a spice market, drifting past piles of scent and colour. A crackling fills the air. Electricity. Tinny voices bounce through the laneways of the bazaar. A woman looks up at the sky and smiles.*

I go down to the lake at dawn, before an Indian-summer heat hits, walk over the rush of the Gardiner Expressway to the tranquility of The Boulevard Club. I clamber over a fence and walk to the breakwall and I lie on it, watching mist skimming over the surface of the water. I'm at eye level with it, and there isn't a breath of air. The water is solid, impenetrable as concrete, clear, like ice, and the mist is like huge wisps of snow blowing over it, skittering away from the heat of the sun's rays hitting the water as it rises over the tops of trees. The mist is moving like a series of snakes slithering alongside each other, twisting, turning in an unexpectedly unhuman manner, all together, all at once. Away from me, across the water, trapped in a beam of brightening heat, its only escape up, then, into the air in tornado-like funnels. Beautiful. Circular.

And then the mist is gone. A blink of an eye, a quick turn away, a minute flash of thought of something else, and come back and it's gone. As though the infidelity of a brief glance elsewhere made it disappear. Like I've imagined the whole thing, not a trace of mist left; the air is suddenly warm and I cannot fathom it. I lie there and watch for another half hour, waiting, willing it to come back, but it never does, so I just keep replaying it over and over in my head.

*postcard*

**(Nowhere in particular):** *If you were to pluck a blossom from a honeysuckle bush, pinch the closed end and pull, the tiniest thread would separate from the flower. On the very tip of the thread there would be, unsteadily poised, a drop of clear nectar. And if you were to run the thread over your tongue and place the blossom between your lips, gently sucking, you would taste summer. And if you were to do that while sitting in warm sand, on dunes that stretch out to a cold ocean that sports a bank of translucent, salty haze, you would know exactly where I am today.*

# Acknowledgements

"binary" appeared in *The Fiddlehead*'s Summer 2007 issue. "Ice Out" was published in *grain*'s Autumn 2005 issue, and "Etching" in *Prairie Fire*'s spring 2006 issue. All three appeared in *Coming Attractions 07* (Oberon Press, 2007). The Russell Banks quote in "binary" was taken from the novel *The Sweet Hereafter* (HarperCollins, 1991). The poem cited in "Etching" is "Pomegranate," by Michael Crummey, published in *Salvage* (McClelland and Stewart, 2002). Photographs in "The Offing" were taken by the author and Walter van Broekhuizen.

This book has received an unfathomable amount of support. Many thanks to the Toronto Arts Council, the Edward F. Albee Foundation, the Anderson Center for Interdisciplinary Studies, the Banff Centre for the Arts and Alan Nathan.

Thanks also to Chris Koentges, Greg Hollingshead, Mark Jarman, Gregg Orr, John Pass, Theresa Kishkan and Melanie Little for very close and wise readings, and to Michael Crummey for saying the one thing that made *postcard* what it is. Valiant friends and critics, all.

To Walter and Laszlo I can never say enough thanks (but can always try).

## Also by the author

*A Fork in the Road*
*Saudade: The Possibilities of Place*

ANIK SEE is a Canadian writer who divides her time between Canada and Amsterdam. She is the author of *Saudade* (Coach House Books, 2008), a collection of essays on landscape and possibility, and *A Fork in the Road* (Macmillan, 2000), an account of journeys undertaken by bicycle. Her writing, both fiction and non-fiction, has appeared in many journals and magazines, such as *Brick, Prairie Fire, The Fiddlehead, Geist, grain, The National Post, Toronto Life,* and, as a contributing editor, in *Outpost Magazine*, and has been nominated for numerous awards, as has her printing and design work.